She stood mesmerised by the tether of his touch, by the intense blue of his gaze as it held hers.

It was as if the busy, bustling world of the hospital had faded into the background, leaving them isolated in a bubble that contained memories of private moments—intimate moments only they knew about. Her heart kicked against her breastbone as his finger drew closer to her scalp. She could smell his aftershave. It wasn't one she recognised, but it was underpinned with his all too familiar smell: musk and soap and healthy potent male.

'Do you want to know why I came back after so long out of the country?' he asked.

She drew in a breath that felt as if it had thorns attached. 'To further your career,' she said. 'That's always been your priority. Nothing comes before that.'

He uncoiled the strand of hair and tucked it behind her ear. 'A career is not everything, Mikki,' h̶ ̶ ̶ ̶ ̶ ̶ ̶ ̶ ̶ ̶ ̶ ̶ ̶ ̶ ̶ed back dov̶ ̶ ̶ ̶ ̶ ̶ ̶ ̶ ̶ ̶ ̶ ̶ ̶ ̶ ̶m at nig̶

Dear Reader

All my Medical™ Romance titles to date have had a hero and heroine meeting for the first time within the first pages of the novel. But this time I wanted to revisit a failed relationship—a very popular theme I have explored several times in my Modern™ Romance titles.

The things that draw a couple together can often be the very things that tear them apart further down the track, and so it was with Mikki and Lewis. Their whirlwind affair in London tragically came unstuck and Mikki ran back home to Australia, to all that was familiar.

But time has passed and their paths cross when Lewis comes to work as a leading neurosurgeon at St Benedict's, where Mikki is an ICU specialist. Their careers are closely entwined, but so too is their history. The spark is still there, but can Mikki risk heartbreak all over again over the unreachable Lewis Beck?

As brooding heroes go, Lewis has it all. He's a loner, aloof, in control and needs no one. Or does he?

Mikki is just the person to bring Lewis into contact with his feelings. It is only she who can reach that dark, secret place inside him where he has stored all the hurt, guilt and grief and disappointments that life has dished up. I loved watching their second chance at love unfold. It was an emotional journey for me writing it as I know many people do not get the second chance they hope and pray for.

I hope you are deeply touched by their story.

Melanie Milburne

THE SURGEON SHE NEVER FORGOT

BY
MELANIE MILBURNE

MILLS & BOON

First published in Great Britain 2011
by Mills & Boon, an imprint of Harlequin (UK) Limited,
Eton House, 18-24 Paradise Road, Richmond, Surrey TW9 1SR

© Melanie Milburne 2011

ISBN: 978 0 263 88599 6

Harlequin (UK) policy is to use papers that are natural, renewable and recyclable products and made from wood grown in sustainable forests. The logging and manufacturing process conform to the legal environmental regulations of the country of origin.

Printed and bound in Spain
by Blackprint CPI, Barcelona

Melanie Milburne says: 'One of the greatest joys of being a writer is the process of falling in love with the characters and then watching as they fall in love with each other. I am an absolutely hopeless romantic. I fell in love with my husband on our second date, and we even had a secret engagement—so you see it must have been destined for me to be a Harlequin Mills & Boon author! The other great joy of being a romance writer is hearing from readers. You can hear all about the other things I do when I'm not writing and even drop me a line at: www.melaniemilburne.com.au.'

**Melanie also writes for
Modern™ Romance!**

'THE FIORENZA FORCED MARRIAGE
by Melanie Milburne: insults fly, passion explodes,
and it all adds up to an engaging story
about the power of love.'
—*RT Book Reviews*

To my niece Claire Elizabeth Luke.
You are a beautiful person inside and out.
Love you. xx

With special thanks to Dr David Rigg
at The Royal Hobart Hospital, an intensive care
specialist who was very generous with his time
in helping me research some aspects of this novel.
His dedication to his patients really moved me deeply.
Thank you.

CHAPTER ONE

IT WASN'T that Mikki hadn't expected to run into him at some point, she just hadn't thought it would be quite like this. She had thought it through in her head: she would be in the doctors' room, he would come in and she would look up, as casual as you please, and act as if what had happened between them seven years ago had never occurred. Or, alternatively, she would be in ICU, attending to one of the patients under her care, when he would come in. She would be all cool and professional, treating him exactly the same as she would treat any other specialist at St Benedict's.

But not like this. It wasn't supposed to be like this. This wasn't how she had planned it at all.

As soon as she stepped into the restaurant she saw him. In spite of the subdued romantic lighting there could be no mistaking that tall rangy, dark-brown-haired figure. He was sitting alone at a table towards the back of the restaurant, his concentration on the menu in front of him, but then, as if some internal radar of his had picked up her presence, he raised his head and his startling ice-blue eyes met hers.

Mikki felt like someone had landed a punch in her belly. The air gushed out of her lungs. She couldn't breathe. She couldn't move. She stood with her eyes locked on his, her heart going into a painful spasm for endless moments until she vaguely registered that someone was speaking to her on her left.

'Dr Landon?' the *maître d'* said at her elbow. 'Your mother called to say she would be ten minutes late. Shall I show you to your usual table?'

Mikki turned and forced a polite smile to her stiff lips. 'That would be fine. Thank you, Gino.'

The *maître d'* pulled out her chair for her and she sat down on legs that felt as spindly and ungainly as a newborn foal's. She kept her head down, making a business of turning her mobile phone to the vibrate setting before she sat back with an ease she was nowhere near feeling. She daren't look across at the other table but she could feel the weight of that penetrating all-too-critical, all–too-assessing gaze.

Was he thinking how much she had changed since she had seen him last? Her honey-brown hair was longer now; she had gone from the urchin look of her early twenties to a more sophisticated shoulder-length style that was easy to manage given the long and often unpredictable hours she worked. She was certainly thinner than seven years ago. Her approach to exercise had been very ad hoc in the past. Now she was an addict, or so her mother kept telling her. Mikki didn't necessarily agree or disagree. She exercised to keep her demons at bay and the pay-off was a figure she had longed for and had never achieved until now.

'Hello, Mikki.'

The deep, smooth bass of his voice with its hint of a London accent brought her head up and her heart rate beyond anything it had ever done in a spin cycle class. Mikki looked into those Antarctic eyes and felt the cold breeze of his disdain blow holes in her chest like a volley of bullets. 'Hello, Lewis,' she said, pleased her voice sounded so cool and composed when for a moment she had thought it might not work at all.

His eyes moved over her face, pausing for an infinitesimal moment on her mouth, before coming back to her gaze. 'How are you?'

'Um—fine, and you?' Mikki felt her facade slipping. Why had he looked at her mouth like that? That one brief glance had set off a chain reaction beneath the surface of her lips. They felt dry and tingling and she desperately wanted to moisten them with her tongue but somehow fought the urge.

She drank in his features in one quick slurping glance: his dark brown hair had only a few strands of grey in it, although he was now thirty-six years old; and his body, although lean, was well muscled, suggesting he also spent a bit of time in the gym. His sensual mouth was deeply grooved either side with vertical lines that in a lesser man would have been aging but in Lewis's case gave him a distinguished, knowledgeable and eminently commanding air. He still had a prominent scar over his right eyebrow, the result of a fight when he had been a teenager. He had never told her the circumstances of it; he had said it was a part of his past he was not proud of, and in spite of her probing had refused to be drawn on it.

'Dining alone this evening?' he asked, glancing at the empty chair opposite.

'No, I'm...' She hesitated, wishing she was meeting

one of her colleagues at the very least, or a date. A date would have been better. Much, much better. 'I'm having dinner with my mother. She's running late.'

One of his dark brows moved upwards ever so slightly. 'Please give her my regards,' he said. 'I don't suppose she has forgotten me?'

How could anyone ever forget you? Mikki thought with a pang that felt like a tiny fish hook in her heart. 'Of course not,' she said. 'I told both my parents you were coming to St Benedict's to join the neurosurgical team. They were interested in how well your career has gone.'

'Surprised would be more appropriate, don't you think?' he asked with that same mocking lift of his brow.

Mikki reined in her temper behind a cool impersonal smile, holding back emotions that were straining at the leash of her control. There was no way she was going to show how much seeing him again had rattled her. 'You were always going places, Lewis. No one could have doubted that.'

'Ah, darling, I can't believe I'm *so* late,' Heloise Landon said as she came in on a cloud of perfume and the rapid tattoo of click-clacking designer heels. 'You would not believe the traffic, and Rashid, my driver, had trouble starting the car— Oh!' She gave a little shocked gasp. 'It's not Lewis, is it? Lewis Beck?'

Lewis held out his hand, hardly a muscle moving on his face. 'Heloise. You're looking well.'

Heloise's perfectly manicured hand fluttered back to her neck once he had released it. 'My goodness,' she said. 'How long has it *been*?'

'Seven years,' he said with an expression as unreadable as stone.

'Yes, of course,' Heloise said. 'Well, this is rather a coincidence, I must say. Fancy running into you like this! I've heard all about your appointment at St Benedict's. It was in the paper and, of course, Michaela confirmed it. Not that she's let too many in on the secret, mind you. I had to drag it out of her and I'm her mother.' She gave Lewis a you-know-what-she's-like look. 'But, then, I don't suppose it is de rigueur to go brandishing about the news of one's ex-fiancé's imminent arrival just because you're going to be working with him every day now, is it?'

Mikki wished the floor would open up and gulp her down whole. She chanced a glance at Lewis's expression but it remained inscrutable, although she thought she saw a glint of something hard in his eyes as they briefly encountered hers. Again, she kept her own expression cool and composed, although it was taking more of an effort than she could ever have imagined.

Heloise was undaunted. 'Won't you join us? You can tell us all about your stellar career. That would be lovely and civilised, don't you think, darling?' She addressed the latter comment breezily to Mikki.

Mikki had grown to dread her fortnightly dinner sessions with her mother, and would ordinarily have jumped at the chance of diluting her company, but the thought of sharing a meal with Lewis was beyond her capabilities right now. 'I am sure Lewis has other arrangements for this evening,' she said a little tightly.

'Yes, I have, actually,' Lewis said, nodding towards the young woman who had just been led to his table. He encompassed Mikki and her mother in one look that was polite but indifferent, and added, 'Maybe some other time.'

The hook in Mikki's heart dragged a little bit further when she saw him greet the gorgeous young woman who had been shown to his table. His arms went around the young woman's slim figure, almost lifting her off the floor as he held her to him. Mikki knew it was ridiculous of her to be feeling so wretched at seeing him with someone else. Of course he would have someone else by now. He would have had many someone elses over the last few years. She should have prepared herself better for a situation like this. She had been concentrating on the work part, the professional, not the personal, when the personal was the thing that hurt the most. It shouldn't, but it did, even after all this time.

Mikki turned away before she saw his mouth go down on that pretty rosebud mouth. 'So, how are you, Mum?' she asked.

'Michaela,' Heloise said, leaning forward conspiratorially, 'did you see that girl he has with him? Why, she's barely out of her teens, I'm sure of it.'

'Yes, well, he always did go for the young innocent type,' Mikki said as she examined the wine list with studious intent.

'Darling, you were twenty-two,' her mother said, 'hardly a babe in the woods.'

Mikki brought her head up from the wine list and sent her mother a wry look. 'I thought you and Dad said I was too young to know what I was doing and I was just about to throw my life away on my first real love affair.'

Heloise pursed her mouth before she spoke. 'He's done very well for himself, hasn't he?'

'What are you saying, Mum?' Mikki said as she began perusing the wine list again. 'That I made the biggest mistake of my life in leaving him when I did?'

There was a tense little silence.

Heloise let out a frustrated breath. 'Michaela, you're always *so* defensive. Of course you did the right thing in leaving him. You had nothing in common with him.'

Mikki put the wine list down and met her mother's gaze. 'I loved him, Mum. I thought that was all the common ground one needed.'

'But, darling, did he love you?' Heloise asked. 'There's a very big difference between lust and love, you know.' She took one of Mikki's hands across the table and stroked it gently. 'I know losing the baby was hard but in the end it worked out for the best, didn't it?'

'Yes, yes, it did.' Mikki pulled her hand away and tried to ignore the sharp pain she always felt when the subject of the baby she had lost came up. She had felt so ashamed of letting her parents down. Her first trip abroad on her own and look what had happened. Her well-to-do parents' hopes for their only daughter to one day have a society wedding with all the trimmings had been pushed aside for plans for a shotgun affair in a London register office, sandwiched between procedures in one of Lewis's theatre lists.

'Do you know if he's married?' Heloise asked, leaning back in her chair. 'I didn't notice a ring, did you?'

Mikki had looked but was not going to admit to it. 'I have no idea.'

'Do you think that's his mistress?' Heloise asked. 'Rich and powerful men nearly always have mistresses, don't they? It seems to all be the rage these days.'

Mikki put the wine list down again with a heavy sigh. 'Look, Mum, I don't care who it is. Lewis has a perfect right to see who he likes. It's none of my business.'

Heloise shifted in her seat like a hen ruffling its feathers. 'I don't want to argue with you, darling. I'm just trying to make conversation. You seem so stressed lately. And your father told me the last time he had lunch with you, you barely ate a thing. Is something wrong?'

'Of course there's nothing wrong,' Mikki said. 'I've just been putting in some long hours.'

'You work too hard, darling,' Heloise said. 'Why do you drive yourself into the ground? Don't you think you need a bit of a balance? You're not getting any younger.'

'Twenty-nine is the new nineteen, Mum, didn't you know?' Mikki said dryly.

Her mother pursed her mouth again and reached for her wineglass. 'You can joke about it all you like, but when was the last time you went on a date?'

'I went out to dinner with a colleague the other day,' Mikki said.

Heloise narrowed her eyes. 'That was a work thing, wasn't it? And didn't you tell me there were four other people there? Hardly what I would call a date, darling. When was the last time you were kissed?'

'Mum!' Mikki kept her voice low but her colour was high. 'Will you please butt out of my love life?'

Heloise gave her an affronted look. 'Only trying to help, dear. No need to bite my head off.'

'Sorry,' Mikki said, feeling her shoulders slump. For years she had worked incredibly hard at her career but she had come to a point just lately when her high-stress, high-responsibility job was not enough any more. She wanted more from life than long hours and a six-figure income. But it was so hard to put a toe in the dating pond when she had almost drowned all those years ago.

'You're not on call, are you?' Heloise asked as Mikki took a sip of the wine the waiter had just poured to refill their glasses.

'No, not tonight,' Mikki said. 'I was on last weekend.'

Mikki wanted to look across at Lewis's table. She ached to have one more look at his face, to see if he was smiling at his date, to see if his eyes were crinkling up at the corners the way they used to do. Not that he had smiled a lot in the past, but when he had, it had been in a way that had made his rare smiles all the more valuable and meaningful. When he smiled his eyes lost that hard ice look and took on a summer-sky tone instead.

She wanted to reacquaint herself with the look of his hands, with those long, tanned fingers with their dusting of masculine hair, those clever, amazing hands that had saved so many lives, the hands that had touched her and caressed her and held her. She wanted to look again at his mouth, the mouth that had kissed hers so passionately, the lips that had touched her in places she had not been touched since.

Heloise's glass clinked against the side plate as she placed it back on the table. 'Don't frown, Michaela. You'll get wrinkles.'

Mikki forced her expression to relax. 'Sorry, I was just thinking about work.'

'Have you heard from your father since he arrived in Paris?'

'Yes, he called me last night.'

Heloise reached for her glass again and took a sip of wine. 'Did he tell you he is thinking of marrying Rebecca?'

Mikki put her glass down. 'He did, actually. How do you feel about it?' she asked, studying her mother's features. Her parents' divorce a couple of years ago had not really come as much of a surprise. They had grumbled along for years, not really happy together but neither of them unhappy enough to leave, until her father had met someone working for his international investment company.

Heloise gave a relaxed smile. 'I'm happy for him.'

Mikki frowned. 'But Rebecca is so much younger than him. What if they decide to have children? She'll want them surely?'

'Darling, your father always wanted more children but I was unable to have any more after you,' Heloise said. 'I think it's lovely that he's got another chance. Rebecca is a sweetheart. She'll make a lovely mother. Maybe I'll get the chance to babysit. I would love that.'

Mikki was still frowning so hard her forehead ached. 'I can't believe you're so accepting of all this. I would want to move to another side of the world instead of...' She stopped, suddenly realising what she was saying.

'How will *you* feel if Lewis suddenly introduces a wife and family to you?' Heloise asked with a pointed look.

Mikki had to drop her gaze in case her mother witnessed the pain she felt at the prospect of seeing Lewis

with a little brood of his own. No one at th...
had said much about him other than mention...
his appointment in the neurosurgical department a...
Benedict's was one of the most exciting appointments
in a long time, but, then, she hadn't exactly gone fishing
for information. 'I imagine I will cope with it,' she said.
'I was the one who walked out on him, not the other
way around.'

'Was it hard, seeing him again?' Heloise asked after
another little pause.

Mikki picked up her wine and gave her mother what
she hoped was a convincing smile. 'Not at all,' she said.
'As far as I'm concerned, he's just another colleague
working at St Benedict's.'

'But you'll see rather a lot of him, won't you, given
that he's a neurosurgeon and you're in ICU?'

Mikki had lain awake at nights thinking about exactly that: how she would cope with seeing Lewis on a
daily basis. His patients would become hers. They would
have to consult each other on management and care.
There would be ward rounds and joint interviews with
relatives, staff meetings, and the shared space of the
doctors' room. It would be next to impossible to avoid
him, and if she tried, someone would surely notice and
comment on it. It was going to be hard to pretend he
was just like any other colleague but she was determined
to do it. 'Don't worry, Mum,' she said, taking another
fortifying sip of wine. 'I'm not going to fall for Lewis
Beck again. That part of my life is definitely well and
truly over.'

CHAPTER TWO

'HAVE you met the new neurosurgeon yet?' Kate Fry, one of the recovery nurses, asked Mikki a couple of days later.

Mikki continued writing in the patients' notes as she spoke. 'Not formally. What's he like?'

'Gorgeous,' Kate said in a dreamy tone. 'Tall, at least six-four, with the most amazing piercing blue eyes. And get this: he's not married.'

Mikki put the file on the top of the others on the desk in the doctors' office waiting to be filed. 'Do you have Mrs Bronson's file there?' she asked. 'I have to check on her potassium levels.'

Kate found the file and handed it to her. 'Apparently he was engaged briefly a long time ago, back in London. I wonder what broke him and his fiancée up. Have you heard any gossip?'

Mikki made a note in the file and handed it back. 'I am not sure Mr Beck would appreciate having his private life discussed on the ward,' she said curtly.

'No one can hear us in here,' Kate said, undeterred. 'I can't imagine breaking up with someone like him, can you? He's über-exy.'

'If you go for the aloof, show-no-emotion type,'

Mikki said in a disinterested tone as she picked up another file to leaf through.

Kate gave a little gulp. 'Er...I'd better get back to the
ward. See you later.'

Mikki felt the hairs on the back of her neck lift up
follicle by follicle. She turned round and met the inscrutable gaze of Lewis from where he stood in the
doorway. 'Apparently you've made quite an impression
on the female staff,' she said, keeping her voice even
and controlled.

The corner of his mouth lifted but it was still not
quite a smile. 'Not all the female staff,' he said. 'Have
you been actively avoiding me, Mikki? I haven't seen
you since we ran into each other at the restaurant the
other night.'

Mikki felt the pull of his gaze and had to drag hers
away with an effort. 'Of course I haven't been avoiding
you,' she said, keeping her voice low in case any of the
other staff were about.

'I didn't see you at the welcoming morning tea,' he
said.

She straightened the already straight papers on the
desk. 'I was busy with one of the patients, that's why.
You know what ICU is like. There is always the possibility of a crisis of some sort.'

He leaned back against the filing cabinet with in-
dolent ease, as if he had been working there all his
professional life instead of having arrived two days ago.
'What have you told people about us?' he asked.

Mikki gave her head a little toss as she faced him.
'Nothing.'

One brow lifted in an arc. 'So no one knows we were once engaged?'

'Why should they?' she said.

The corner of his mouth kicked up again. 'Interesting.'

Mikki felt her lower back tingle as his gaze swept over her, lingering a little too long on her mouth. Again her lips began to fizz with sensation and she ached to send her tongue out to dampen down their sudden dryness, but it seemed to be too intimate an action, a signal of want and need she wasn't prepared to reveal at any cost. It wasn't supposed to be like this. She was supposed to be professional and mature about this situation, not fluttering with nerves and panic every time she ran into him. 'Have *you* told anyone?' She threw his question back.

'Not yet.'

Mikki wasn't sure what she felt about his 'not yet'. It seemed to contain a threat that he might at some point reveal their past relationship. A couple of people at the hospital knew she had been engaged once but she had never told anyone Lewis's name or occupation. She didn't want anyone to connect the dots, and certainly not now with him here in the flesh. 'What about your girlfriend?' she asked. 'Surely you've told her about your broken engagement?'

He folded his arms across the broad span of his chest, his eyes still holding hers in a lock-down that was as penetrating as it was unnerving. 'Abby is not my girlfriend,' he said.

Mikki only just managed to stop from rolling her eyes. 'Well, whatever she is, she's clearly smitten by you. She was hanging on every word that came out of your mouth.'

His eyes softened. 'She's rather sweet, isn't she? I'm sorry I didn't introduce you but we had a lot of catching up to do.'

'I'm sure you did,' Mikki said crisply.

There was a little beat of silence.

'So how are we going to manage this situation?' Lewis asked.

'You mean working together?'

'Yes. Are you going to be OK with it?'

'I'm perfectly fine with it,' Mikki said, but on the inside she was screaming, *Of course I'm not OK with it!*

'That's fine, then,' he said, unfolding his arms.

Mikki pressed her lips together. 'Um—what about the other stuff?'

His brow lifted again. 'What other stuff?'

'The we-were-once-engaged stuff,' she said.

'I don't see that it has anything to do with anyone but us.'

Just to hear him say 'us' was enough to send a shock-wave of reaction through her whole body. To be bracketed with him in such a way was deeply disturbing. It suggested an intimacy between them that should no longer be there. *Was* it still there or was it just her imagination? It was hard to tell from his expression. Even when they had been together in the past he had revealed little of himself. He had been an island she had briefly visited before pulling up anchor and moving on.

But how soon before the hospital grapevine got its tentacles around their past? The medical world was small, the subset of the surgical world even smaller. It would only take one word out of place for people to make the connection. 'Well, I'm not about to tell anyone,' she said. 'I make it a habit to keep my private life separate from my professional one.'

'You've done well career-wise, from all accounts,' Lewis said, pushing his hands into his trouser pockets as he crossed one ankle over the other. 'No one works longer hours, or so I'm told. That can't keep much time free for a private life.'

Mikki shifted her gaze out of the range of his. 'I love my job.'

'You say that as if you're trying to convince yourself rather than me.'

She threw him a cutting look. 'I don't suppose you've cut back to working nine to five these days?'

His ice-blue eyes glittered like shards of ice. 'I've been working on the work-life balance.'

Her expression showed her cynicism. 'I'm sure you have.'

'Are you seeing anyone?'

Mikki frowned at him. 'What sort of question is that?'

He gave a light shrug. 'I'm interested in what my successor is like. Or has there been more than one?'

'It's been seven years,' Mikki said with a lift of her chin. 'What do you think?'

Something moved in his eyes, a camera-shutter flick. 'You're not married.'

She arched her brow. 'So?'

'And you're not living with anyone,' he said.

Mikki folded her arms, the height of her chin

challenging. 'You seem to have done your homework. The question that begs to be asked is: why? Why are you so interested in my private life after all this time?'

Another beat of silence ticked past.

'Was it worth it, Mikki?' he asked. 'Have you finally got what you want?'

Mikki dropped her arms from around her chest and moved to the other side of the office, her eyes averted from his. 'Of course I've got what I want,' she said.

'And yet you don't seem happy.'

She swung back to face him angrily. 'You're overstepping the mark, Lewis.'

'Am I?'

She tightened her mouth. 'You know you are. My happiness or lack thereof should be of no concern to you.'

'Is that the way you want to play this?' he asked. 'Just pretend we don't have a history together? How long do you think it will be before someone finds out? Sooner or later someone's going to make the connection, Mikki. We worked in the same hospital in London. You know how the system works. Everyone knows everyone in this profession.'

Mikki swallowed a knot of tension in her throat. 'No one needs to find out if we maintain a professional distance.'

He gave a snort of mock amusement and drawled, 'You're fooling yourself, sweetheart.'

Mikki cast a nervous gaze around to see if anyone had overheard his casual endearment. 'Don't call me that.'

He stepped closer, his tall frame shrinking the space

like an adult stepping into a child's cubby house. 'It's still there, isn't it?' he said in velvet-smooth tone.

Mikki didn't need to ask him to clarify what he meant. She could feel it in the air between them— the tension, the crackling, the energy, the temptation. 'You're deluding yourself, Lewis,' she said. 'I've moved on. We've both moved on with our lives.'

One of his hands picked up a strand of her hair that had worked its way out of the tight ponytail she had fashioned earlier that day. He coiled it around his finger in an action he had done so many times in the past. Mikki couldn't have moved away if she had tried. She stood mesmerised by the tether of his touch, by the intense blue of his gaze as it held hers. It was as if the busy, bustling world of the hospital had faded into the background, leaving them isolated in a bubble that contained memories of private moments—intimate moments only they knew about. Her heart kicked against her breastbone as his finger drew closer to her scalp. She could smell his aftershave. It wasn't one she recognised but it was underpinned with his all-too-familiar smell: musk and soap and healthy potent male.

'Do you want to know why I came back after so long out of the country?' he asked.

She drew in a breath that felt like it had thorns attached. 'To further your career,' she said. 'That's always been your priority. Nothing comes before that.'

He uncoiled the strand of hair and tucked it behind her ear. 'A career is not everything, Mikki,' he said as his hand dropped back down by his side. 'It can't keep you warm at night.'

Mikki stepped out of his force field. 'I'm sure you

have plenty of nubile companions to do that for you,' she said.

He gave that almost-smile again. 'You sound jealous.'

She sent him a gelid look. 'I can assure you I'm not.'

'All the same, it would be good if we can be friends as well as colleagues,' he said. 'I don't want to add to the stress of the workplace by us being at war with one another.'

'Friends, Lewis?' Her expression was incredulous. 'Isn't that asking a little too much given the circumstances?'

His jaw grew tense as if he was trying to contain the anger that was there just under the surface of his civility. 'You walked out on me, Mikki,' he said. 'You didn't give our relationship a chance.'

Mikki glared at him. 'Our relationship should never have occurred in the first place. It was a mistake from start to finish.'

'I know it had a rough start but we could have worked at it,' he said. 'We could have tried to sort out the career commitments so that both of us could have had what we wanted.'

'We didn't want the same things,' Mikki said. 'You never wanted the ties of a family so early in your career. You told me that when we first met. But then, when I told you I was pregnant, you turned into someone else. You were obsessed with the baby, what school it would go to, what football team it would support, which of us it would look like. How could I know if you were truly enthusiastic or just making the best of a bad situation?'

'What was I supposed to do?' he said. 'Abandon my

own flesh and blood? I couldn't do that. There was no other choice but to get married. I got you pregnant. It was my fault. I accepted that then and I still accept responsibility for it now. I didn't want any child of mine growing up without its father.'

Mikki felt perilously close to tears, tears she hadn't shed in years. 'You were glad when I lost the baby. I know you were. It left you free to get on with your life without the responsibility of parenthood to deal with.'

'Why would I be glad that you had to go through that?' he asked, frowning darkly. 'What sort of jerk do you take me for? I was gutted when you lost the baby.'

'You never said a word to me,' Mikki said. 'Why didn't you say something?'

'You had been through a devastating experience,' he said. 'I didn't think it was fair to dump my stuff on you on top of what you'd gone through. Talking about it only makes it worse, or that's what I thought at the time. I hated seeing you cry. I felt responsible. I was the one who got you pregnant. I felt like I had ruined your life.'

Mikki bit her lip. She was feeling shocked at hearing his side of things. She had been so focussed on what she had felt that she hadn't factored in Lewis's feelings at all. He had always been so composed and clinical. Had he hidden all that he was feeling behind that mask of professional composure? Had he truly felt as devastated as she had?

Lewis scraped a hand through his dark brown hair, leaving deep grooves in the strands. 'I don't do emotion well, Mikki,' he said in a world-weary tone. 'For work I have to shut off my feelings so they don't cloud my judgement. It's hard to switch them back on again in my private life.'

His private life was a sore point and it made her sound a lot more resentful than she would have liked. 'You didn't seem to have too much trouble accessing your feelings the other night with Gabby or Tabby or whatever her name was,' Mikki said.

'You really are spoiling for a fight, aren't you, Mikki?' he asked.

Mikki opened her mouth to send him a scathing retort but he had already swung away to walk out of the office, almost bumping into one of the registrars as he left the ward.

'Gosh, Mr Beck seemed rather annoyed,' Kylie Ingram commented as she came into the office. 'Has one of his operating lists been cancelled or something?'

'I'm not sure,' Mikki mumbled by way of reply, before excusing herself to answer her mobile.

'We have four patients scheduled to come in tomorrow for Mr Beck's list,' Jane Melrose, an ICU nurse, informed Mikki as she came in for her shift a couple of days later.

'Have we got the beds?' Mikki asked, frowning as her gaze swept over the already full unit.

'Not unless someone is transferred, discharged to the ward or dies,' Jane said flatly.

Mikki pressed her lips together. 'Then Mr Beck's list will have to be culled. We're stretched to capacity as it is and that's not leaving room for any A and E admissions.'

'I'll call the theatre supervisor,' Jane said and sighed. 'Remind me why I work here?'

'You get paid,' Mikki said.

'There's got to be more to it than that,' Jane said. 'Aren't I supposed to feel fulfilled and get a sense I'm making a difference?'

Mikki smiled. 'We're all making a difference, Jane. I'll call the theatre supervisor. You go and have your tea break.'

Jane instantly brightened. 'I just remembered why I work here. You are such a nice person to work with.'

'It's very sweet of you to say so, Jane, but I have a feeling I'm not going to be popular once I've made this call,' she said as she resignedly picked up the phone in the office.

'What do you mean, half my list has been cancelled?' Lewis snapped at the theatre supervisor who had delivered the news.

'I'm sorry, Mr Beck, but there are no available beds in ICU,' the nurse said. 'Dr Landon was most insistent.'

Lewis frowned. 'So this was Dr Landon's decision?'

'Well, sort of, I guess,' she said. 'This stuff happens all the time. ICU is always full to the brim and the op lists have to be shuffled around a fair bit. If there's no ICU bed post-op, you can't operate. Some of ICU is contracted out to the private hospital next door, but the unit is too small anyway.'

'I know how a co-located hospital works,' Lewis said curtly. 'I just don't like having decisions made over my head without consultation with me. Which patients were cancelled? I should be the one deciding which patients are put off, not someone who has never seen the patients. I know who is the most urgent, I've done the work-ups, organised the preparation. I will be the one making that decision.'

'You'll have to take up that with Dr Landon,' the nurse said, giving a nervous grimace before she left.

Lewis scraped a hand through his hair in frustration. He didn't like being the ogre with nursing staff but his first week and a half at St Benedict's hadn't gone as smoothly as he would have liked. His office and consultation room were still being painted and fitted out, even though he had been promised they would be ready by the time he arrived, and now half his operation list had been cancelled by his ex-fiancée. Was she deliberately putting him in his place or was there a genuine bed crisis?

He went down to the unit but Mikki was nowhere in sight. He asked one of the registrars on duty, who informed him she had gone to the doctors' room on the fifth floor for a coffee break.

Lewis took the stairs two at a time and shouldered open the doctors' room door to find Mikki waiting for some fresh coffee to brew in the percolator on the bench next to a microwave and toaster. 'Just the person I want to see,' he said, pressing the door with the flat of his hand so it clicked shut.

Her tawny-brown eyes widened a fraction. 'I take it this is about your list?' she said.

'I have four ill patients I need to operate on tomorrow,' Lewis said. 'What am I supposed to say to them now you've cancelled the surgery on half of them?'

'We haven't got the beds,' she said. 'The two we've

given you don't need ICU beds post-op. Didn't Theatre Management tell you?'

'Find the beds,' he said, locking gazes with her, his mouth set in an intractable line. 'I want those two operations to go ahead as planned.'

'I can't do that. The unit is full. We had two unexpected admissions from private overnight. That's the two post-op beds gone. I'm sorry, but that's just the way it is.'

'Mikki, this is ridiculous,' he said. 'Surely there is a better way of managing this? Those two beds should have been earmarked for neurosurgical post-op. The private hospital should have sent their patients elsewhere. Aren't there any patients you can transfer to another ICU somewhere else? Is there not one patient here you can wean off a ventilator?'

'I can't turn people's ventilators off just because you need the beds,' she said with a spark in her eyes.

'I'm not asking you to do any such thing. There should just have been better communication over this, especially with me.'

'Look, Lewis, the system is overstretched here. They should have told you that before you took on the position,' she said. 'It's like this just about every week with every surgical speciality in need of high-dependency beds. There just aren't enough ICU beds for every specialty. People have to be postponed, especially, it seems, public patients.'

'Mikki, you know neurosurgical patients are nearly always high acuity,' he said. 'Surely I don't have to bargain for beds every time I'm scheduled to do a list?'

Her eyes moved away from his as she poured her

coffee. 'Take it up with the hospital management,' she said. 'It's not my problem.'

'Have you even thought about a way to manage this better?' Lewis asked.

She turned her defiant brown gaze on him. 'It's my job to keep critically ill patients alive. I don't have the time to brainstorm on how to manage the hospital better. That's Administration's job.'

'How many non-surgical patients do you currently have in ICU?' Lewis asked.

'Seven.'

'How many of them are on ventilators?'

'Two.'

'Then why can't those other five patients be transferred somewhere else and free up ventilated beds?' he asked.

She appeared to think about it for a moment. 'That would take a hell of a lot of organisation, transferring patients between ICU units in different hospitals. There would be issues, infection control for a start. But I doubt if Admin would come at the transfer costs, even if we could find other non-surgical ICUs willing to take patients.'

'There are private hospital ICU beds elsewhere. Non-ventilated beds could be leased there to free up post-op beds here,' he said.

She put her coffee cup down. 'That's something that would have to be dealt with by the powers that be. I can only do what I can to make room in my own department.'

'Mikki, I would really appreciate if we could some-how just do this,' Lewis said. 'I have a thirty-five-year-old mother of three who has already had a subarachnoid bleed from an aneurysm. If she has another bleed, for which she's got a worse than fifty per cent chance in the next day, she won't make it—three kids with no mother. The other urgent patient has an astrocytoma on the verge of coning. If I don't debulk the tumour asap it's not going to be worth doing. And I think the new regime of intracranial chemo and radical radiotherapy has a real chance of eradicating this tumour. Twenty-one years old. Think about it, Mikki. This young guy hasn't even started life and he's staring down the barrel of it ending if I don't do this operation. I'm not being difficult just for the heck of it. I really want those cases done. This is what I've spent the last decade training to do, and because of some dumb administrative lethargy I'm being told I can't treat these people.'

Her slim throat rose and fell. 'I understand the urgency. I always try and accommodate the high-priority cases. But I'm up against a limit here. I'm not the head of the department. Jack French is.'

'But he's currently on leave. Surely you can take charge here, can't you? Someone has got to.'

'Yes, I know.' She gave a sigh of resignation. 'I'll see who I can possibly move but I'm not making any promises.'

'That's my girl,' Lewis said.

'Not any more,' she said with a little hoist of her chin as she moved past him. The door closed behind her, the click of the lock adding a measure of finality to her statement.

Lewis had to fight his primal response to go after her. His reaction to seeing her again was something he had been preparing himself for ever since he had been approached about the position at St Benedict's. It had been one of the reasons he had taken the post. He wanted to prove to himself he had moved on. He had known it would be difficult, seeing her. He had known it would stir up old hurts and disappointments. But he hadn't expected to feel the same level of attraction after all this time. It had caught him totally off guard, which was foolish of him now that he thought about it. Over the last seven years, whenever he had thought of Mikki and their short and passionate time together he had felt a deep aching sense of loss at how it had ended. He had been in and out of other relationships before and since but he had never felt anything when he thought about them or even when he occasionally ran into them. But with Mikki it was like a punch to his gut, a deep, cruel punch that ached and throbbed for hours afterwards. This posting was supposed to change all that. To de-sensitise him, but so far it was doing the opposite.

Normally he was good at locking away his feelings. Since his brother's death twenty years ago, feelings had been off limits. Feelings equalled vulnerability. And the one thing he hated to show was any sign of vulnerability. Mikki had walked out on him, so showing any sign of hurt, betrayal or disappointment had been the last thing he had been prepared to do. But somehow seeing her again had triggered something deep inside him and he couldn't seem to turn it off. It niggled at him, like an annoying itch he couldn't reach to scratch. She evoked feelings in him he had never expected to feel for anyone again. He didn't want to need her. He didn't want to want her. He had never wanted to want or need her or anyone.

But just as she had come into his life in the past she had changed his black and white to vivid vibrant colour with her sparkly personality and endless cheerfulness. He had seen very little of that vibrant personality since he had come back. Had he done that to her with his clumsy handling of their relationship?

He felt the bone-deep ache of desire when he was with her, a physical need that no other woman incited in him. Somehow standing within touching distance of Mikki made him want to pull her into his arms the way he had had all those years ago and feel her body nestle up against his as if she had finally found her way home. He had not felt that with anyone else. It annoyed him that he hadn't moved on as far as he had thought. Was it the fact that she had ended their relationship and not him? Hadn't she just reminded him of it with her pert response?

She was no longer his girl.

She was no longer his lover.

She was no longer his fiancée.

He didn't matter to her any more. That was what hurt the most. It was the one thing he couldn't move on from. He was a part of her past she clearly wanted to forget. The fact that she hadn't mentioned it to anyone suggested she was ashamed of it. That hurt. That really, really bugged him. What they'd had together had been good, better than good. They'd had the chance to have a wonderful partnership and she had thrown it all away. How could she have professed to have loved him so passionately way back then but feel nothing for him now?

It shouldn't matter what she felt now, but it did. And that was perhaps the thing that annoyed him most. He *wanted* her to still feel something for him, anything but that cool professional show-no-emotion ice-princess thing she had going. He was determined to break through it. He would chip away at that icy barrier until he found the warm-hearted, spontaneous girl he had fallen in love with seven years ago.

He just hoped she was still there...

CHAPTER THREE

'Wow, Mr Beck must have really laid down the law with you,' Jane Melrose said as she saw the orderlies in the process of transferring two patients to other hospitals.

Mikki gave her a speaking glance. 'He can be very persuasive. But to tell you the truth, he has a point. This place could be better managed.'

'Jack French won't want to hear you say that,' Jane said. 'He thinks he's the best director this unit's ever had.'

'He does the best he can,' Mikki said. 'But it's always complicated. Look at poor Mrs Yates, for instance. Eighty-seven years old, on a ventilator with no sign of improvement after her bile-duct injury. Her daughters want us to withdraw support but her son is refusing to allow it.'

'I think it's about her will.' Jane said. 'I heard one of the relatives talking about it. Apparently she changed it recently and the son wants it changed back. Fat chance of that happening. Greedy vultures, some people.'

'You certainly see the best and worst of human behaviour in here,' Mikki said with a sigh.

Jane cocked her head at her. 'Hey, do you know what I heard when I was on break?'

Mikki kept her voice cool and disinterested. 'I have no idea.'

Jane swung back and forth on the ergonomic chair. 'Mr Beck has bought a house in Tamarama overlooking the beach. Do you reckon it's that house you were telling me about, the big one across from you where that soap actress used to live with her boyfriend before they moved to Hollywood?'

Mikki felt a feather of suspicion dance up her spine. 'I did happen to notice a "Sold" sign on it when I got home yesterday but I have no idea who the new owner is.'

'That'd be cool, being neighbours with Mr Beck, don't you think?' Jane said.

Mikki tried to keep her face and her tone blank. 'I can't imagine why anyone would think that would be cool.'

Jane stopped swinging to look at her. 'Don't you like him, Mikki?'

Mikki gave an up-and-down lift of her shoulders. 'He's all right, I guess.'

'He's more than all right,' Jane said. 'My heart flutters every time I see him. I'd love him to ask me out. Maybe I'll make the first move. I know some men don't like that but what have I got to lose?'

'I think you'd be wasting your time,' Mikki said. 'He's already got a girlfriend.'

'Has he?'

'Yes, a dark-haired gorgeous woman who looks like she could be a model,' Mikki said, feeling the pain all over again as she thought of that bone-crushing hug Lewis had given his date.

'How do *you* know?' Jane asked, looking at her with intrigue.

'I saw them when I had dinner with my mother. They were dining in the same restaurant.'

'Well, that's a shame,' Jane said, flopping back in her chair. 'Why are all the good ones already taken?'

'It's life,' Mikki said wearily, and reached to answer her ringing phone.

After Mikki spent a good hour in the gym she drove home to her little town house squeezed in between the exclusive mansions in a cul-de-sac in the beachside suburb of Tamarama. It was going to take a lifetime to pay off, but it was wonderful to be within walking distance of the ocean. The briny smell of the sea and the rolling waves cleared her head as nothing else could. She loved standing on her small balcony and watching for dolphins in amongst the die-hard surfers who were in the water no matter what the season.

In spite of living there for well over a year now, she hadn't got to know any of her neighbours all that well. She stopped to chat to one or two of them now and again, but the hours she worked made socialising a little difficult and her free time was so precious she mostly spent it alone or at the gym. As for dating, well, that had been an area of her life that had never quite got off the ground after she'd returned from London. She'd had dinner a couple of times with a friend of a friend just recently but nothing had come of it. It was intensely annoying but every time she went out with another man she couldn't help comparing him to Lewis. It was as if Lewis was her benchmark of what she felt to be the ideal man. Everyone else fell short, if not in height, then in looks and personality and intelligence.

It wasn't that she still felt anything for him, well, nothing she was prepared to openly admit. In her most private moments she allowed herself to unlock that door in her heart where she stored that still weeping wound. Was love supposed to hurt for this long? Surely by now she should have forgotten about him and moved on.

When she had heard he was coming to Sydney to take up a position at St Benedict's she had been furious. What right did he have to come waltzing back into her life, even if it was only professionally? That was how she had fallen for him in the first place. She had been a medical student on rotation in London, the same hospital where Lewis had been doing his registrar training. The irony was they hadn't met at the hospital but in a pub frequented by homesick Aussies. She had come in out of the rain just as he had been going out. She had almost stabbed him in the stomach with her umbrella and he had stolen her heart with his ghost of a smile.

It had been a whirlwind romance, or at least for her. Mikki suspected Lewis had been used to a rapid turn-over of bedmates. He was very experienced, but looking back she realised that had probably been in comparison to her inexperience.

She had been so terribly young and naive, so fresh faced and enthusiastic about life. She had fallen hard for Lewis, very hard. He had been her polar opposite. She had been bubbly and happy and he had been dark and brooding and serious. She had loved their differences. She'd loved making him smile. She'd taken it on as a mission to make him laugh out loud. She had never achieved it but she had made those lips of his curve upwards at her and his amazingly blue eyes dance a little.

Lewis had always seemed so controlled and in control. He hadn't needed anyone. He'd had no one to need. His mother had died when he was young, and his father when he'd been a teenager, which had left him with no extended family to speak of. For someone who'd craved others' approval so much, Mikki had found his air of untouchable aloofness devastatingly attractive. His lone-wolf status had intrigued her. She had been unable to imagine having no one in her life to lean on, but he had always shrugged off any notion of regret about being without a family.

Their first meeting had turned into a date, and then another. Within days of meeting they were sleeping together. She told him she loved him the third week they were together, a spontaneous gushing confession that to this day still embarrassed her. He had not said he loved her back, at least not then. He had just given one of his half-smiles and ruffled her hair, as one would do to a small, over-enthusiastic child. He made no promises but, then, why would he? He knew she was only in the UK for three months. Lewis made it clear he was staying in the UK and Europe for an indefinite period. He had no plans to return to Australia. What chance did they have of a permanent relationship when they were going in different directions?

That point was driven home to her almost daily as he barely acknowledged her at the hospital as he always seemed so determined to keep his private life separate from his professional one. At first Mikki admired his commitment to his career. The neurosurgical pathway was a demanding one. The long hours of difficult operations and arduous study left little time for play. She knew it and accepted it but still she secretly longed for more than he was prepared to give.

She was already neglecting her studies in those first few weeks of being blissfully in love but she felt it was worth it. Lewis was worth it. How he made her feel was worth any sacrifice. But then finding out she was pregnant turned her world upside down. All her career plans took a sudden nosedive. Lewis was shocked at her news but he was determined to do the right thing by her and the baby. He insisted on marrying her as soon as it could be arranged. Mikki had wanted more time to think about taking such a big step. She believed marriage was a lifetime commitment and she had always dreamed of doing it properly. She felt too young. She felt unprepared for all marriage and a baby would entail. Her reluctance to marry in a rush caused many a heated argument, some of which had gone on for days. There never seemed to be enough time to resolve anything. The phone was always ringing with another emergency or a patient needing urgent care. Lewis was a diligent and very capable registrar and the specialists trusted him to do the footwork for them, which he did without question and without complaint. He seemed to thrive on the challenges work threw at him. He relished the difficult cases, working on his skills alongside some of the best-known names in the field.

But Mikki felt Lewis had changed after finding out he was going to be a father. Their relationship changed. She could never put her finger on exactly how it was different, but the subtle change of mood increasingly made her feel as if he was only staying with her out of a sense of duty. Yes, he had said he loved her after she had told him about the baby. He had even said he had been going to say it days earlier but had wanted to find the right time. She wanted to believe him and did for a time. But then the doubts crept in, like shadows under a door. Those shadows lengthened as time went on, reminding her of the precarious position she was in, loving a man much more than he loved her.

After losing the baby, her decision to call off the wedding seemed the only sensible thing to do. Mikki could see Lewis was distancing himself since her miscarriage. They spent no time together, instead passing through the flat like flatmates who barely knew each other. She was preparing herself daily for him to call the wedding off himself but for some reason he didn't say a word. She lived in a constant state of unease, a feeling of impending doom that destroyed her self-confidence even further.

Her parents, who had flown over the week before, had already spent the whole time they had been there trying to get her to change her mind about going ahead with the marriage. She didn't want to be influenced by her parents, but neither did she want to make a mistake that would have repercussions for the rest of her life. She thought long and hard about leaving Lewis, but once she had made up her mind it was relatively easy to put the necessary steps in place.

Her parents had taken a couple of days to visit the Cotswolds and arranged to meet her at the airport the following evening when Lewis was on night shift. Mikki left a note and closed the door on their shoebox-sized flat with a sound that still echoed deep within her heart...

One of the regular dog walkers was coming along the footpath as Mikki collected her mail from the letter-box. She smiled at the middle-aged woman called Margery and reached down to pat the fluffy, pint-sized canine. 'Hi, there, Muffy. You're not pulling on your lead today. Those obedience classes must be working.'

The dog's owner laughed. 'Yes, they are,' she said. 'She was the most improved last session.'

'That's very good to hear,' Mikki said, smiling.

'The house across the road from you has finally been sold,' Margery said. 'Have you met the new owner?'

'Not that I know of,' Mikki said, wondering if that was true now or not. 'Have you?'

'No, but I heard it was bought by another doctor from St Benedict's. A specialist of some sort, I've forgotten which one. I thought you might know him.'

'No doubt I will run into him some time,' Mikki said, prickling with annoyance.

'I think it's nice for the neighbourhood to have some more professionals in residence,' Margery said. 'I hope he brings a wife and family with him. After all those all-night rave parties with you know who, it will be a nice change to have some young children about the place.'

Mikki exchanged a few more desultory words before going up the path to her town house. She didn't like where her thoughts were taking her. She was being paranoid. Why should she immediately think it had been Lewis who had bought that stunning and incredibly expensive house? At least a hundred doctors worked at St Benedict's. Any one of them could have purchased the property. It was in a great location, and it was certainly relatively close to the hospital, which was essential if one was in one of the more emergency based specialities where time was so important.

Mikki tried to put it out of her mind as she went upstairs to shower and change out of her gym gear. She had only just dried and dressed when the doorbell sounded. She flicked back her still damp hair and padded down the stairs, and even though she had a security camera screen to check who was at the door, she didn't use it. She didn't need to. She knew exactly who was there and why.

'Lewis,' she said as she opened the door. 'Just the person I want to see.'

'Well, sweetheart, I'm deeply touched,' Lewis said dryly. 'You're just the person I want to see too.'

She flashed him a furious glare. 'You'd better come in. I wouldn't want your future neighbours to take a set against you before you even move into the neighbourhood.'

One of his dark brows winged upward. 'So you've heard about my little purchase across the road?'

Mikki shut the door with a sharp click as he stepped over the threshold. 'What is this?' she asked. 'First you come to work in the same hospital I work in, you eat in the same restaurant I eat in and now you're moving into the same street. What's going on?'

'Nothing's going on,' he said. 'I was headhunted for the post at St Benedict's.'

Mikki placed her hands on her hips and angled her head at him in suspicion. 'And the restaurant?'

'It's the most popular restaurant on that stretch of Bondi.'

'And the house?'

He gave her a winning smile. 'It was a steal. Do you realise how much I would have had to pay for a similar property in London?'

She rolled her eyes at him. 'There are no beaches in the centre of London so I'm not quite getting the comparison.'

'It's a nice house.'

Mikki clenched her hands into fists. 'It's right across the street from mine!'

He gave her a guileless look. 'So?'

She blew out a breath of frustration and fury. 'So what were you thinking?' she asked. 'It's bad enough I have to see you every day at work.'

'I thought you said it wasn't going to be a problem for you at work,' he said.

Mikki swung away towards the kitchen, her bare feet slapping against the polished floorboards in anger. 'You could have had least told me about the house when we were speaking earlier today,' she said. 'I can only imagine you didn't because you knew I'd be furious.'

'I don't get why you should be furious about me living in the house across from you,' Lewis said. 'I need a place to live. It was for sale and it ticked all the boxes.'

She turned back, sending him another lightning flash of hatred. 'Do you think I want to see you bringing home your brainless bimbos at every hour of the night?'

A muscle twitched at the side of his mouth but not in amusement. 'Don't look if you don't want to see.'

Mikki felt like a pressure cooker was about to burst inside her. All her anger, all her hurt and pain was bubbling out of control. She had to get a grip on herself. She was acting like a heartsore spinster who had regrets over abandoning her wedding banquet. Very Dickensian, only she was the one who had done the jilting. She turned away to compose herself. 'Why are you here?' she asked after a long, tense moment.

'I wanted to tell you about the house but obviously the grapevine at the hospital got there first.'

She gave a huffy movement of her shoulders as she faced him again. 'Fine, so you've bought a house. Congratulations. Don't expect a house-warming present from me.'

'You're making this situation a whole lot worse than it should be,' he said. 'Surely we can talk about things without tearing strips off each other.'

Mikki didn't know what to make of his expression. Hard to read at the best of times, it gave no clue to what was behind the glacial screen of his eyes. But, then, he had always held himself together so well. She had often felt he had a wall up that separated him from the rest of the world. No one could get to him and he couldn't or wouldn't reach them. 'I'm not sure what there is to talk about,' she said. 'In fact, I'm not even sure we should be talking at all outside the hospital.'

'You don't think we can manage some sort of amicable relationship in spite of our history?' he asked.

She gave him a searing look of disdain. 'What it is about men that they think they can just carry on as if nothing has changed? *Everything* has changed, Lewis. I don't know you any more. In fact, I don't think I ever truly knew you in the first place. We're as good as strangers now.'

'Then why not just start afresh?' he said. 'Let's pretend we just met and take it from there.'

Mikki narrowed her gaze. 'What exactly are you suggesting?'

He came over to where she was standing, stopping just in front of her, not touching but close enough for her to feel pull of attraction that just wouldn't go away. It was alive in the air, a third presence in the room, a disturbing presence that reminded Mikki of every erotic intimacy they had ever shared. Her eyes zeroed in on his mouth, dragged there by a force she could not resist. His lips were so familiar and yet so foreign. She had once known every contour of that mouth. She had felt its fire and passion on every part of her body. She had known every inch of his body; she had explored it in intimate detail. Her hands had felt every bunching muscle, her fingers had felt the throb and swell of his arousal, and her mouth had tasted his essence. She had lain in his arms for snatches of time that lived on in her memory no matter how hard she tried to forget them. Her body tingled with the rush of memories; her skin came alive with the need to feel his hands on her once more. Could he sense it? Had she somehow communicated it to him non-verbally? If so, she had to pull herself into line. She had to get control. She wasn't supposed to still love him after all this time.

It had to stop.

Right here.

Right now.

Lewis held out a hand to her. 'Hi, my name is Lewis Beck.'

Mikki blinked a couple of times before she slowly put her hand in the warm enclosure of his. 'Um—hi, I'm Michaela Landon.'

He released her hand. 'Nice to meet you, Michaela.'

Mikki put her still tingling hand back by her side. 'Um—everyone apart from my parents calls me Mikki,' she said, feeling foolish but going along with it anyway. It was weird, surreal almost. They were repeating practically verbatim the words they had exchanged on that first meeting all those years ago in that London pub. Did he realise it? she wondered. Was it deliberate?

'So what are you doing for dinner?' Lewis asked. 'Do you fancy grabbing a bite to eat somewhere?'

OK, so it had to be deliberate, Mikki thought. 'I was going to have leftovers,' she said, breaking the sequence. 'There's only enough for one.'

He acknowledged that with a hint of a rueful smile. 'Just as well you said that because I'd forgotten what came next.'

'What came next was I said I didn't usually go out with complete strangers,' she said.

'That's right, and then I said we weren't exactly strangers because we were both Aussies.'

'And then I asked you what you did for a living and we realised we worked at the same hospital,' Mikki said.

'And then I said that settles it, we're not strangers but colleagues so having dinner together would be perfectly appropriate,' Lewis said. 'So, how about it?'

The question hung in the air for long moments like a resounding echo from the past.

Mikki bit down on her lip as she lowered her gaze from the piercing blue of his.

'You know, I think you did that way back then too,' Lewis said in a low, gruff-sounding tone. 'It made me want to kiss you then and there.'

She looked up at him, her heart suddenly pounding as she saw the way his eyes flicked to her mouth before coming back to her gaze. This was heading into dangerous territory. She could feel it. She could feel the spell of remembering the good times weaving its magic around her, making her think of the pleasure just one kiss from his mouth would evoke. But where would one kiss lead? He wouldn't stop at one kiss any more than she would want him to. It was a temptation she would have to resist.

She was supposed to be demonstrating how she had moved on with her life. She had thought she *had* moved on until she'd seen him again. Seeing him in person was so different, so emotionally wrenching and deeply unsettling. She felt confused. Nothing seemed so cut and dried as it had before. She had always thought that because he hadn't come after her when she'd left, it had proved he hadn't loved her. But what if she had misjudged him? She of all people knew he was proud in an aloof, untouchable way. His I-don't-give-a-damn approach to what people thought was something she had always secretly admired. She was the total opposite, often crippled by the fear of what other people would think or say about her.

She didn't know how to maintain her equilibrium

when he looked at her with those intense blue eyes that saw so much and yet gave so little back. Could he see how tempted she was to revisit the past? It was an ache inside her, a pulsing ache to feel his arms around her, to feel his hard body respond to hers the way it had done while they had been together.

She had to be strong.

If she tumbled straight back into his arms, what would that say about her? Wouldn't it prove she had wasted the last seven years of her life? And what would happen when it was over, as it surely would be once he reverted to his old, distant, show-no-emotion ways?

She swallowed the restriction in her throat and forced herself to step out of the magnetic range of his presence. 'Game over, Lewis,' she said. 'I don't remember much else.'

'I remember how soft your lips were when I kissed you,' he said. 'And that little sigh you gave when I put my arms around you to pull you closer.'

'Stop it,' Mikki said, clenching her hands into fists. 'Will you stop it, for God's sake? I don't want to be reminded of what a silly little fool I was to fall for all those moves you made on me.'

'I remember the first time we made love,' he said as if she hadn't spoken. 'I had never made love with a virgin before. I probably wouldn't have gone ahead with it if I'd known.'

Mikki stamped her foot and pointed to the door with an arm that would have been rigid with anger if it hadn't been shaking so much. 'Get out. Get out now before I call the police.'

His eyes held her stormy ones in a tussle she knew

she could never win. She let out a shaky breath and
swung away, her arms going across her middle to keep
the pain of the past from bending her over double.
'Please leave...' she said raggedly. 'Please, Lewis, just
leave...'

He came over and stood behind her. She felt him
there, the wall of his body like a fortress she could
neither enter nor lean on. She prepared herself for his
touch, every nerve tightening, every cell of her body
alert, and the entire surface of her skin lifting in a shiver
of longing so acute she felt dizzy with it.

'Mikki, Mikki, Mikki,' he said softly as his hands
came down on her shoulders.

She bit back a gulping sob, fighting for control, for
immunity, for anything.

He slowly turned her round to face him, his eyes
locking on hers, his hands gentle and warm on her bare
skin. 'I shouldn't have come here like this,' he said. 'But
I was checking something at the house and I saw your
lights on.'

Mikki bit her lip to stop it from trembling. She
didn't trust herself to speak; her voice was locked in
her throat, caught up behind a wall of emotion that had
been bricked in there for years.

'I guess I thought if we had a talk away from the
hospital it might clear the air,' he said. 'I don't want this
enmity between us. We should be able to move past it
by now.'

'I have moved past it,' she said hollowly.

He brushed the side of her mouth with one of his
thumbs, a tender caress that set her lips aflame. 'I didn't
intend to hurt you the way I did, Mikki,' he said. 'I

shouldn't have got involved with you in the first place. We were from different worlds; you have no idea how different. I should never have allowed it to go as far as it did but at the time I just couldn't seem to help myself.'

Mikki had never heard him speak like this before. He had never expressed regret or remorse in the past. When they had argued she had been the one to apologise. He hadn't taken any responsibility for disagreements or upsets. He had always made her feel as if she was the one in the wrong for expecting too much, for demanding more than he was prepared to give. It had made her doubt herself to the point that she had bent over backwards to keep the peace, losing herself and her dreams and aspirations in the process. 'Why are you telling me this now?' she asked.

His hands dropped from her shoulders. 'As soon as I was approached about the position at St Benedict's I knew it would have implications if I took the job,' he said. 'I'd heard you were working there. I didn't think it would be a problem until I saw you at the restaurant that night.'

Mikki frowned. 'How did you expect me to react? To welcome you with open arms or something?'

'No, of course not,' he said. 'I just didn't realise you still hated me that much.'

She moved away to put some distance between them. 'Lots of once involved couples have to interact with each other due to ongoing work or family commitments,' she said. 'My parents are a shining example of how it's done. I am sure we will be able to come to some arrangement where the past no longer matters.'

'I heard about their divorce,' he said. 'That must have been hard on you.'

Mikki gave a shrug, still without looking at him. 'I saw it coming for years. They're happier apart than together. My father has a new partner. He's thinking of getting married to her. My mother thinks it's great.'

'So you'll be cool about seeing me with other women if the occasion arises?' Lewis asked.

Mikki was glad she wasn't facing him. 'Of course,' she said. 'As long as you are cool with seeing me with other men.'

The silence swelled for a moment with something she couldn't quite identify.

'Why did you buy the house, Lewis?' she asked, turning to face him. 'The real reason.'

He looked at her for a long moment. 'This area has a special meaning for me. I have a lot of memories of surfing along this part of the coast.'

Mikki frowned. 'I never knew you surfed.'

'I don't,' he said. 'Not any more.'

'I guess you didn't get much chance in London.'

He gave a slight smile that twanged on something in her heart. 'No.'

Another little silence while their eyes still held each other's beat after beat after beat.

'I guess I should let you get on with your evening,' he said, looking away. 'I won't be moving in for a couple of weeks, maybe a month. I want to get some work done on the house first. I hope the tradesmen don't disturb you too much.'

'I'm sure it won't be a problem. I'm at work most of the day in any case.'

'Right, then,' he said. 'I'll see myself out. No, stay there. I know where the front door is.'

Mikki stood and watched him leave, her emotions in turmoil. She was confused and agitated, unsettled by his uncharacteristic confession of remorse over their past. Was he easing his conscience so he could move on with his life or had there been some other agenda?

CHAPTER FOUR

THE first of Lewis's patients arrived in ICU later the next day. Mikki had seen the young woman's husband and three children waiting outside the unit for a couple of hours. She always tried to keep a clinical distance but sometimes, especially when children were involved, she found it just that little bit harder. The eldest of the three children was no more than six; the middle one was still in pull-ups; and the baby was exactly that—a baby of not more than six months. The husband looked like most husbands would in that terrifying situation. He looked haggard and ashen in colour; his eyes hollow with damson-coloured smudges underneath them, as if he hadn't slept since his wife had been diagnosed.

'Hi, I'm Dr Mikki Landon,' she said, holding out her hand to him. 'I'll be looking after your wife in ICU. We've got her settled now. Would you like to come in for a brief visit? We're keeping her well sedated and on the breathing machine for a few days while the recovery from her surgery is occurring, and she's doing pretty well at the moment.'

'Thank you,' Mark Upton said, hustling the two older kids together as he picked up the baby in her capsule in his other hand. 'I'd like to thank Mr Beck too but he's still in Theatre. He saved Jenny's life. I want to thank him personally. Will he be around later to check on her?'

'I'm certain he will,' Mikki said. 'He's had a few difficult cases today but he shouldn't be too far away now. It's a bit crowded around an ICU bed and all the tubes and machines can be daunting, so can I get our ward clerk Marianne to get the kids a drink and sit in the interview room with them while you go in for a few minutes?'

'Thanks, that'd be good. Jenny's mother is just about here to take the kids home.' Mark bent down to talk to his little troop of bug-eyed children. 'Kids, Daddy's going in to see Mummy after her operation. She's asleep now and we don't want to wake her, so I'll go in and kiss her goodnight for all of us. A lady called Marianne is going to get you a drink and Grandma is coming to take you home for dinner.'

After kissing and hugging each child, and reassuring them again before he handed them over to the ward clerk, Mark followed Mikki into ICU.

Lewis came into the unit still dressed in theatre scrubs. Mikki's heart gave a little leap. He looked so tall and in control, the master of his universe—confident, competent and commanding. She watched from another patient's bedside as he stopped to talk to Mark Upton. The children had been collected earlier by Jennifer's mother but Mark hadn't left his wife's side for hours. Jennifer was progressing as well as could be expected, but it didn't escape Mikki how close the young mum's brush with death had been. If a bed hadn't been made available as Lewis had demanded, that poor family would quite possibly now be without their mother. Everyone on the unit was talking about the ground-breaking surgery Lewis had performed. Apparently two other neurosurgeons had refused to operate on the young mother as they thought it was too risky. It didn't surprise Mikki that Lewis had put his hand up for the task. He had developed a reputation as a maverick amongst his colleagues, breaking new ground, developing new techniques that offered hope where previously there had been none. It didn't always make for a comfortable position in the department or in the surgical community at large. Some of his colleagues would no doubt feel he was stepping over their boundaries, or showing them up, but privately Mikki admired him for mastering his skills, taking them to the next level, challenging himself all the time to bring the best patient care possible.

Mikki went back to the office to write up the drug chart on her other patient when Lewis came in a short time later. She put her pen down and swung the chair round to face him. 'Everyone is talking about the miracle you pulled off with Jennifer Upton,' she said.

'There wouldn't have been a miracle without the bed you made available,' he said. 'She's doing well so far but it's still early days.'

'I really feel for the husband and the kids,' Mikki said. 'They look so terrified.'

'Yes, it's been a tough time for them.'

He wrote something on in a file with a look of deep concentration on his face. Mikki couldn't stop looking at him; her eyes were drawn to his features—the line of his mouth, the bridge of his nose, his scar across his eyebrow and the stubble on his jaw that she longed to reach out and touch.

He suddenly looked up from the file. 'Is something wrong?' he asked.

Mikki felt her face flush with colour. 'No, of course not. I was just thinking how tired you look.'

'Yeah, well, it's been one of those days,' he said. 'Ten hours in Theatre that should have only been eight but the anaesthetist was painfully slow, and the nursing staff changed with just about every patient.'

'I guess you have to get used to working in the public system,' she said. 'It might not be so frustrating in private practice when everyone is champing at the bit to get the work done and get home after it's done, and of course there's no teaching.'

'Well, it was my decision to come back to Australia and work primarily in the public system,' he said with a self-deprecating twitch of his mouth.

'Why did you come back?' Mikki asked. 'It can't just have been about your career. You had all that and more in the UK.'

His eyes held hers for an infinitesimal pause. 'I liked it in London. I hated the climate at times, but I liked the work and the people I worked with. But I wanted to come back home to see if I could make a difference here. I felt I owed it to my country. That patriotic enough for you?'

'You never struck me as a particularly patriotic sort.'

'You don't think I would lay down life and limb for my homeland?'

'I would hope you wouldn't have to.'

'I very nearly did when I spent a couple of months in a field hospital in Afghanistan.'

Mikki felt the sudden lurch of her heart. 'You were in Afghanistan?'

'Yeah, it was pretty grim at times,' he said. 'But it was a good feeling, being able to do something for the cause.'

'Were you in danger?' she asked, feeling a hollow sensation in her stomach.

'Had to dodge a few bullets and bombs now and again but a lot less than the men and women in the forces have to deal with, especially in trying to protect me from blundering into some dangerous situation.'

'How can you be so casual about it?' Mikki asked, frowning as she thought of him injured, or worse. 'You could have been killed.'

He closed the folder and dropped it on the desk, his eyes containing a hint of irony as they met hers. 'And that would have upset you why exactly?' he asked.

Mikki opened and then closed her mouth, not trusting herself to speak. She couldn't rid her mind of an image of his long body in a flag-draped coffin like so many others. How close had he come to losing his life? How could she not have known about it? Sensed it? She could not imagine the world without him in it. She suddenly realised she didn't want to be in a world without him in it.

The silence ticked along with the clock for a moment or two.

'Do you know why I offered my services?' Lewis asked.

She shook her head. 'No... Why did you?'

'I told myself at the time that I needed a new challenge,' he said. 'But after what happened out there I realised what I had really been doing was running away. But you can't run away. You just can't leave it all behind. It's taken me this long to understand that you take your stuff with you wherever you go.'

Mikki swallowed a prickly lump in her throat. 'What happened out there?'

'I narrowly missed a roadside bomb,' Lewis said on an outward breath. 'I saw two men lose their lives right in front of me. It kind of made me think: Who would miss me if I was gone?'

Mikki felt that painfully tight spasm of her heart again. 'I am sure loads of people would miss you—your colleagues, for instance.'

'Seven years has gone past, Mikki,' he said. 'Have you missed me?'

Footsteps approached and Kylie Ingram, the registrar, came into the office. 'Sorry to interrupt,' she said, encompassing them both with a smile. 'I have the tickets here for St Benedict's Children's Cancer Ward Ball. I'm not sure if you've heard about it, Mr Beck. The invitations went out a few weeks ago. It's not too late to come. It's this Saturday.'

'I'll have a look at my calendar and let you know,' Lewis said, and moved out of the office.

Kylie handed Mikki the ticket she had ordered. 'Aren't you going to bring a partner, Dr Landon?' she asked. 'You've only bought one ticket but I can easily rustle up another one for you. We always keep a couple of spares just in case.'

'One will be fine,' Mikki said, wishing she had never agreed to go in the first place.

Kylie looked in the direction Lewis had gone before turning back to Mikki. 'Mr Beck is an amazing surgeon,' she said. 'I was lucky enough to be in Theatre with him today. He's a hard taskmaster but he gets the job done. I learned so much from watching him. I think he's going to be great for this place. He's got so much expertise and experience.'

'Yes, he certainly has,' Mikki said, and placed the ticket in the pocket of her coat next to where her heart was still doing its clamp-release, clamp-release action.

'Well, I'm going to head off home,' Kylie said. 'Just let me know if you want another ticket. The ball's going to be a blast.'

Mikki was on her way to the hospital car park when Greg Hickey, one of the orthopaedic surgeons, approached her. They had occasionally met up for a coffee in the doctors' room but she hadn't pursued the relationship further than that. 'Hi, Mikki,' he said. 'I was just about to call you.'

'Is it about Mr Tate?' she asked. 'I left a message on your mobile. He's OK to be transferred back to the ward now the embolus has cleared.'

'Actually, it wasn't about work,' he said with a sheepish look. 'It was a personal thing.'

Mikki adjusted her handbag strap over her shoulder. 'What can I do for you, Greg?' she asked in a guarded tone.

'It's about the ball this Saturday,' he said. 'I was

wondering if you would like to come with me. Kylie Ingram mentioned you were planning to go alone.'

Mikki was about to politely decline his invitation when she saw Lewis coming in their direction. He was speaking on his mobile but he looked across the car park and caught her eye, one of his brows lifting when he saw Greg standing in front of her. She could see the mocking curl of Lewis's lip, which made her angry that he thought he had any sway over her. She gave her head a tiny toss and smiled at Greg. 'I would love to come with you,' she said.

'Great,' Greg said, clearly relieved. 'I hate going to these things alone. Ever since my divorce I've avoided a lot of social gatherings but the registrars and residents have put in a lot of work and I feel I should make an appearance.'

'I know the feeling,' Mikki said.

'I'll pick you up at seven-thirty,' Greg said. 'And thanks, Mikki. I really appreciate it.'

The St Benedict's Ball was an annual event organised by the registrars and residents to raise funds for the hospital. This year it was the Children's cancer ward that was to benefit, and tickets had sold like the proverbial hot cakes. It was to be held in a plush city hotel and over-the-top glamour was the only way to go. Everyone looked forward to dressing up and having fun for a worthy cause. Mikki had only attended a couple of times before, each time without a partner, so it was a new experience to be escorted to the event, even if it was by a man she could only ever consider as a friend, and not a particularly close one at that.

Greg Hickey had not long ago gone through a painful divorce. He had taken his wife's desertion hard, and especially hated seeing his two children only every second weekend. Mikki listened with an empathetic ear as he drove towards the city on the night of the ball. It would be a long night if he didn't change the subject soon but, then, it was going to be a long night in any case, with or without Lewis there. If he didn't turn up she would be thinking all night of what he was doing and who he was doing it with. If he did turn up she would have to watch him with his partner and that would be even worse than her own imaginings.

The hotel was buzzing with activity as they arrived. The ribbon of red carpet led from the foyer and up the grand staircase to where the ballroom was situated. People were milling about with drinks and canapés, everyone looking very different out of their theatre scrubs or hospital uniforms. Mikki walked past three nurses she had worked with in the past without even recognising them. They had a laugh about it, telling her she looked a bit of a Cinderella herself, before moving on to chat to some other guests.

Greg was immediately cornered by a colleague, which left Mikki free to take a glass of champagne from a passing waiter and sip it in peace as she surveyed the crowd. She watched as couple after couple came up the staircase, smiling as she recognised various faces, exchanging a few words with one or two as they drifted past.

One of the last couples to arrive was Lewis and his partner. Mikki felt her heart tighten as she saw the young girl called Abby smiling radiantly as she came up the stairs on Lewis's arm. She was dressed in a cream-coloured satin evening dress that was so like a wedding gown Mikki felt a spike of jealousy pin her to the spot. Would Abby be Lewis's bride some day in the future? The mother of his children? The love of his life?

Greg came back to her side. 'Sorry to desert you like that, Mikki,' he said. 'Shall we go in?' He offered her his arm and she took it with a forced smile.

She walked with Greg to the table they had been assigned, close to the stage where the band had been set up. At least this close to the loudspeakers there would be no possibility of boring filling-the-silence conversation, she thought.

It was impossible not to stare as Lewis led his partner to the table in the centre of the ballroom. He stood a half a head if not more above most of the other men in the room, and he cut such a striking figure in a tuxedo that several women of various ages did double-takes as he took his place after first seating his partner with the solicitous care and attention he had once given to Mikki.

She took another sip of champagne and tried to get her stiff shoulders to relax. She could do this. She had moved on. This was a way of proving it to him, if not to herself. She would tell her mother all about it at their next dinner—how cool and composed she'd been, how *civilised*.

'Lewis Beck's date is rather gorgeous, don't you think?' Greg said as he reached for another bread roll from the basket in the middle of the table. 'I wonder where he found her. He's only been in the country a couple of weeks. Lucky devil.'

'She's far too young for him,' Mikki said tightly.

'I don't know,' Greg mused as he liberally plastered his roll with butter. 'I sometimes think younger women don't expect so much of you as a partner. The ones the same age as you tend to be more demanding. You can never please them.'

'That's because we want to be equals,' she said. 'We don't want a man to look up to like some sort of idol. We'd rather a man be by our side.'

Greg chewed his mouthful of bread before he asked, 'You were engaged once, weren't you?'

Mikki picked up her champagne again. 'It's not exactly common knowledge but, yes, I was, but it didn't work out.'

'Who pulled the plug on it?'

'I did,' she said, looking at the bubbles in her glass.

'It's nearly always the woman who does it, you know,' he said, refilling his glass almost to the brim from the bottle of red wine on the table.

'Does what?'

'Leaves the relationship,' Greg said. 'Most men don't even see it coming. I certainly didn't.'

Here we go again, Mikki thought, but just then the master of ceremonies took the microphone and asked the rest of the guests to take their seats.

The meal progressed and Mikki tried to enjoy what she could of the evening. Greg was surprisingly good company once he forgot about his broken marriage and his bitterness towards his ex-wife. He chatted to Mikki about work and told her about his two children and how much he was looking forward to taking them on holiday to a Queensland island in a few weeks' time.

The band was playing and already several couples were up and dancing. Mikki looked across at Lewis's table and saw Abby tugging at his hand to get him onto the dance floor. He rose to his feet and, wrapping his arm around the young girl's waist, led her out amongst the other couples.

Mikki turned away, biting her lip.

'What's wrong?' Greg said as he leaned in close in order to be heard over the deafening music.

'Nothing,' she said.

'Would you like to dance?' he asked. 'I'm not very good but...' He stopped and rummaged for his phone, which was vibrating in his pocket. 'I'd better get this,' he said. 'It's from my ex.'

She gave him an understanding smile and reached for her evening purse. 'I'm just going to the powder room,' she said. 'Please excuse me.'

When Mikki came out of the ladies' room a few minutes later Lewis was walking down the hall from the direction of the ballroom. There was no way of avoiding him without making it look obvious so she decided to act cool and unaffected instead. 'Enjoying the evening?' she asked.

'You're looking very beautiful tonight, Mikki,' he said, sweeping his blue gaze over her evening dress. 'Black suits you.'

Mikki felt his compliment like a caress on her bare shoulders. It unsettled her, making her tongue sharper than she had intended. 'Where's your date?' she asked pointedly, looking around. 'Or is it already past her bedtime?'

His eyes contained a flicker of amusement. 'She'll party on much longer than I will, I imagine.'

She began to move past him. 'I'd better get back to my table.'

'Your date has left,' Lewis said.

Mikki frowned as she brought her gaze back to his. 'Left?'

'One of the scrub nurses from your table sent me out to tell you,' he said. 'Apparently one of his kids broke their arm while playing at a friend's house. He had to leave in a hurry, presumably to attend to it.'

Mikki chewed at her lip. 'Oh...'

'So how long have you been seeing him?'

'I'm not seeing him, not like you think,' she said. 'He's getting over a very difficult break-up.'

'My heart bleeds.'

She set her mouth and turned again to leave but he caught her by the arm and turned her back to face him. The heat of his touch burned through her bare skin, making her blood race as it simmered in her veins. His eyes locked on hers, holding them in a war of wills she was going to lose. She lowered her gaze to the sensual but steely bracelet of his tanned fingers around her wrist, her heart thudding as she thought of all the times those fingers had touched her in the past.

'Dance with me.' It wasn't an invitation or a request but a command.

Mikki brought her gaze back up to his. 'I don't think that's such a great idea.'

'Why?' he asked. 'Because you might actually enjoy being back in my arms?'

She had to lower her gaze again. 'Please, Lewis, don't make a scene. People are starting to stare at us.'

'One dance, Mikki,' he said. 'We don't even have to do it in the ballroom. We can go out to the balcony where no one can see us.'

Before she could say no he was leading her out an exit to an empty balcony that overlooked the harbour. He shut the door once they were outside, the noise of the ball instantly muffled, as if someone had thrown a heavy blanket over it.

Mikki felt the cool night air on her skin but before she could shiver Lewis had pulled her into his arms and into a slow-moving waltz that stirred her senses into a frenzy of bitter-sweet longing. His hips brushed against hers, and then one of his thighs pushed between hers as he expertly turned her in his arms. She was acutely aware of his hand in the small of her back and the fingers of his other hand interlocking with hers as he guided her around the balcony to the muted strains of the band.

Her body was coming alive in a way it hadn't been in years. Her breasts, already pushed up by her strapless dress, were now also being pressed by the rock-like wall of his chest, the ache she felt for them to be grazed with his teeth and tongue almost unbearable. The fact that her breasts were bare behind the black fabric of her evening dress made her even dizzier with longing. 'We shouldn't be doing this,' she said, hoping he would think she sounded breathless because of the dancing and not his close proximity.

'Why not?' He turned her again with some clever footwork.

'You know why not.'

'We're not hurting anyone,' he said, his breath disturbing the tendrils of hair that were part of her half up, half down hairstyle.

She stared at him. 'What about your date?'

'Last time I looked she was dancing with one of the registrars,' he said.

'Foolish girl,' Mikki said in an embittered tone. 'Somebody should warn her before she ruins her life.'

He stopped dancing and held her close, looking down at her with those intense but unreadable blue eyes. 'Did I do that to you, Mikki?' he asked.

Mikki moistened her lips with a quick dart of her tongue. 'Lewis —I want to go back inside. I don't want people to talk.'

'You're really keen to keep our past a secret, aren't you?' he asked.

'It's better that way,' she said, lowering her gaze to the perfectly aligned bow-tie around his neck. She breathed in his scent, that alluring mixture of citrus, musk and maleness that never failed to stir her senses. Her heart was beating too hard and too fast and it had nothing to do with the dancing. Lewis was standing so close she could feel the swollen ridge of his response to her, the unmistakable arousal that made her blood skyrocket through her body, like rocket fuel in her veins.

'This isn't going to go away,' he said, moving that little bit closer.

'It *has* to go away,' Mikki said, injecting some much-needed determination into her tone, even though she didn't move away from the warmth of his body. She couldn't. She was caught in his force field, trapped by her own treacherous desire.

'I still want you, Mikki.'

The words made her breath stop in her throat like a horse at full gallop suddenly pulled back from a precipice by its rider. She looked into his eyes and felt her stomach turn over. 'Y-you can't mean that,' she said, her voice a breathless rasp of sound.

'I mean it, Mikki,' he said, and brought his mouth down to just a breath above hers. 'And I think it's what you want too.'

Mikki put her fingers against his lips. 'No—wait,' she said, still breathless and whispery.

He captured her hand and kissed each of her fingers, his eyes holding hers as he did so. 'Don't you ever think of how it used to be between us?' he asked.

'No, no, I don't,' she lied.

His lip curled up at the corner of his mouth. 'What are you afraid of, Mikki? That Daddy might not approve of you sleeping with your bad-boy ex-fiancé?'

Mikki tugged her hand away as she shot him a furious frown. 'I fail to see what my father has to do with this conversation,' she said.

He gave her a mocking half-smile. 'Did he tell you he tried to pay me off seven years ago?'

She looked at him as if he had just slapped her, shock rendering her speechless. Her heart was beating so loudly she wondered he couldn't hear it. The sound of it was like an angry ocean roaring in her ears.

'It was a tidy sum of money,' he went on. 'More than I would have earned in a year back then.'

'I don't believe you,' Mikki said but inside thinking, *I don't want to believe you.*

His mouth was still slanted sardonically. 'Barry

Landon wanted his only precious daughter to marry a blue-blood, someone with a pedigree, not end up in a shotgun marriage with some mongrel from the working-class suburbs of Sydney.'

'I admit my father thought I was too young to know what I was doing, and in some ways I agree with him,' Mikki said. 'We hardly had time to get to know one another. One minute we were dating, the next we were expecting a baby.'

'I'm surprised he didn't try and talk you in to having an abortion,' he said.

Mikki couldn't think of a thing to say, which really, in a way, said it all.

His eyes hardened like ice-blue diamonds. 'Did you consider it?' he asked.

'How can you *ask* that?' she said.

'It would have been an easy solution.'

Mikki felt her heart contract. 'Is that what you wanted me to do? You never said anything to that effect. If that's what you were thinking, I think you should know I would never have agreed to it.'

He held her look for a tense moment before he turned away from her and stood ramrod straight, looking out at the view.

It was a moment before he spoke.

A long, long moment.

'No. I didn't want you to do that.'

Mikki ran her tongue out over her dry lips. 'But you didn't really want to be tied down, did you? Not then. It was too early. You had years of study ahead of you.'

He turned back from the balustrade, his face now in shadow, but she knew she wouldn't have been able to read it even if she had been able to see it. 'We should go back inside,' he said. 'Abby will be wondering where I've gone.'

CHAPTER FIVE

THEY had only just stepped back into the hall near the ballroom when Abby came towards them. 'Oh, there you are, Lewis,' she said with a bright, engaging smile. 'I've been looking all over for you.' She gave Mikki an even brighter smile. 'Hi, I've been dying to meet you. Lewis has told me all about you.'

Mikki's polite smile of greeting faltered. 'Oh. Nice to meet you. Abby, isn't it?'

'That's right,' Abby said. 'I'm Lewis's half-sister.'

Mikki's surprised gaze went to Lewis's mask-like face. 'You never said.'

'You never asked.'

She frowned at him. 'I did too. I asked if she was your girlfriend.'

'And I said no.'

'But—but you didn't say she was your half-sister,' Mikki spluttered indignantly. 'I thought you didn't have any family.'

His eyes remained cool and hard and distant. 'I didn't know about Abby until a year ago.'

'It's true,' Abby said. 'My father—I mean *our* father and my mother didn't have me until the year after Lewis had moved overseas.'

Mikki's frown deepened in both confusion and fury as she turned back to Lewis. '*Your father?* You mean to tell me you lied to me about that too? You said you had no parents. What's going on?'

'Er...' Abby held up her hands like someone directing traffic. 'Let's not get into a fight about this. I should have insisted on Lewis introducing us at the restaurant the other night.'

'Why didn't you?' Mikki directed the question at Lewis. 'Or was it because it suited you to have me think you had hooked up with someone as soon as you had arrived back in Sydney?'

His eyes were like cold chips of ice as they held her challenging look. 'I'm a free man and have been for seven years,' he said.

Mikki seethed with anger. 'You could have told me seven years ago you had a father. Why didn't you? Why make me believe you were all alone in the world?'

'As far as I was concerned, I was alone in the world,' he said.

'Can I say something?' Abby interjected.

'No, Abby,' Lewis said sternly. 'Stay out of it.'

'No, I will not stay out of it, Lewis,' Abby said. 'You should have told her. You should have told her all of it.'

Mikki swung her gaze back to the young girl. 'I don't understand. He should have told me all of what?'

'It's all very sad and complicated.' Abby gave a little sigh. 'Lewis's brother died when Lewis was sixteen. Liam was fourteen. My father...*our* father didn't cope well with Liam's death. He married my mother a few weeks after Liam died. It was a pretty miserable marriage. They divorced when I was ten.'

Mikki gaped at Lewis. 'You...you had a brother?'

'Yes.' His face was as expressionless as marble. It was as if he was listening to some banal conversation that had absolutely nothing to do with him. How could he be so distant and unmoved by his own family history?

Abby continued. 'Lewis left home the year before I was born. When I was old enough to understand, my mother told me I had a half-brother who lived abroad but my father was against me making any contact. I got the feeling I wouldn't be received all that well. But then one day I decided it was time to take matters into my own hands. I made contact via email and flew over to London for a visit last year after I finished school.'

Mikki gave Lewis a wounded look. 'Why didn't you tell me?'

'I had left that part of my life behind when I moved to England,' he said. 'I wanted to forget about it and move on.'

Mikki wondered how much she had known the Lewis she had fallen in love with back then. Had it been her fault for not probing further? Why had he neglected to tell her some of the most important details of his life prior to meeting her? Or had there simply not been enough time? Their relationship had been so fast and full on. She had told him a lot about her background, but perhaps by her being so open it had made him feel less inclined to open up about his. After all, hers was a privileged background. He had already alluded to his working-class roots. 'I wish I had known about this...' she said, chewing on her lip in anguish. It explained so much: his locked-down emotions; his insular mentality; his distancing when she'd lost the baby. He had already lost a sibling. How devastating would that have been? He had shut down, pretending it hadn't happened, in order to cope. He had created a new life for himself in another country.

'Um… I think I should make a move,' Abby said, biting her lip as she glanced around.

Mikki became aware of some of the other attendees at the ball milling around, chatting, as the band took a break. She caught sight of Jane standing nearby with a quizzical expression on her face and wondered how long it would be before the gossip started about her past relationship with Lewis. What if someone had heard something on their way past?

'Lewis, would you mind if I left with a friend?' Abby said. 'I promised I'd catch up some time and now seems as good a time as any. We thought we might go clubbing. That's if you don't mind?'

'Of course not,' he said. 'I'll be taking Mikki home shortly.'

'Excuse me?' Mikki gave him a pointed look. 'Don't I have some say in that?'

'Don't argue with me,' Lewis said darkly. 'You're creating a scene.'

'*I'm* creating a scene?' she threw back.

'Um, look, I'm really sorry,' Abby interjected with a worried look on her young face. 'I shouldn't have said anything about Liam. Have I made things horribly worse?'

'No, of course not,' Lewis said. 'I was going to tell Mikki eventually.'

Mikki gave him a sour look. 'When was that? In another seven years' time?'

'I'd rather not discuss this out here in the corridor,' he said through tight lips.

'Um, I really should get going,' Abby said. She turned her gaze to Mikki with a bright and friendly smile. 'Maybe we could hang out some time. I'd like to get to know my big brother's fiancée.'

'*Ex*-fiancée,' Mikki said, throwing a look in Lewis's direction.

'Sorry, yes, of course.' Abby's smile faded. 'I keep forgetting…'

'See you around, kid,' Lewis said, and bent down to kiss Abby on the cheek.

'Thanks for inviting me tonight,' she said, looking up at him adoringly. 'I had a great time.'

'Take care of yourself,' he said in a gruff tone.

'I will.' She lifted a hand in a fingertip wave as she dashed off to join a handsome young man, who was waiting patiently at the top of the grand staircase.

Mikki turned to face Lewis. 'I really can make my own way home,' she said. 'I don't want to take you out of your way or anything.'

His hand came down on her arm, sliding down until he got to her wrist, his long fingers overlapping each other. 'It's no trouble. Besides, I feel I need to explain why I didn't tell you about Liam.'

Mikki blew out a shaky breath as he led her back to the ballroom to collect her wrap. She didn't want to cause any more of a scene, although, judging from the speculative glances coming their way, it was probably too late to avoid the fallout. The hospital grapevine would be running rampant by Monday and there would be nothing she could do to stop it. Her head was spinning with the information Abby had given on Lewis's background. It explained so much about his reluctance to talk about his past. And yet there was still so much she didn't know. How had his brother died? Why had Lewis left the country of his birth, never to return until now? Did he have any contact with his father? Why had he locked that part of his life away as if it had never existed?

Lewis had valet-parked his car and it arrived with a deep, throaty growl as they went down to the foyer. He opened the door for her and tipped the parking attendant before he came around to take his seat behind the wheel.

'You do realise everyone will be talking about us leaving the ball like this?' Mikki said into the taut silence a minute into the journey.

'Let them talk.'

She swivelled in her seat to look at him. 'You really don't give a damn, do you?'

'About some things, yes.'

Mikki sat back and stared at the passing scenery, hardly seeing it as she thought about how he must have felt when her father had tried to pay him to get out of her life. Was that another reason he had said nothing about his past? She had always known they had come from very different socio-economic backgrounds. The arrangements over their wedding had brought that home on more than one occasion. He had said he wanted small and simple, but had he really? He probably couldn't have afforded anything else at the time. Her parents marching in the way they had, trying to take control, had probably made his pride come up. She hadn't thought he was intimidated by the differences in their backgrounds. He had always seemed so unimpressed by the social climbing and name-dropping that went on. It had been another thing she had admired about him.

Her parents had insisted on flying over at short notice once Mikki had told them about Lewis's intention to get married, ostensibly to try and talk her out of it. She cringed now at the thought of how that tawdry little scene must have played out between Lewis and her father. It sounded like something out of a Regency novel: the over-protective, doting parent trying to shield her daughter from certain ruin by getting involved with a man from the wrong side of the tracks.

'Your sister is very beautiful,' Mikki said after a long silence. 'You must be very proud of her.'

'I am.'

'It was very good of you to move all the way back here just to be closer to her,' she said after another pause. 'It must have been a big sacrifice career-wise.'

'Most things we want in life come with some sort of compromise attached,' he said. 'I was happy to make the sacrifice for her.'

'Do you have any contact with your father?' Mikki asked.

'No.'

Mikki looked at him again but he was focussed on the road ahead. 'But surely now you're back here—'

He flashed an icy glance her way. 'It's not something either of us wants or needs.'

'I don't believe that,' she said. 'He's your father. He must want to see you.'

'He doesn't.'

Mikki bit her lip and turned to look at the passing scenery again. It was obviously a no-go area even now. It struck her that if she had known about Lewis's past their relationship might not have ended up the way it had. She had been too young to see how the secrets from his past had cast dark shadows over their relationship. She had blamed him for being emotionless and locked down, but now it all made sense. She thought again of how devastating the loss of a sibling would have been. Why had he not mentioned it? It hurt her to think of how he had locked her out of his innermost pain. Surely if he had cared about her even a little, he would have told her some, if not all of his past?

He had always been such a loner. She had felt sorry for him, although he had brushed off her sentiments at the time. He had said how glad he was he didn't have any relatives to answer to, no one to bend over double trying to please, no expectations to live up to. He had himself and only himself to please. But now he had Abby he had turned his life upside down to be near her. It was such a turnaround. It was like seeing him as another person. Not as a lone wolf but as a lion protecting his family, small as it was. Did that mean he would one day want a family of his own? Was that one of the reasons he had come back to Australia, to put down the roots that for so long had been missing from his life?

Lewis turned into her street—*their* street, she reminded herself with a funny little flutter in her stomach. She waited until he had pulled up outside her town house before she turned to look at him again. 'Would you like to come in for a coffee or something?'

His eyes were in shadow but she felt the full force of his gaze on hers. 'Yeah, why not?'

Mikki could think of a couple of very good reasons why not, but she wasn't brave enough to acknowledge them to herself, let alone out loud.

Lewis helped her out of the car and accompanied her to her front door. Mikki tried not to fumble with the key but her fingers felt like the bones had been disconnected.

'Do you want me to do that for you?' Lewis asked.

She handed him the key without connecting her gaze to his. 'Thanks.'

Once inside Mikki felt even more nervous. It was a bizarre feeling to be alone with Lewis. No work distractions. No colleagues to deal with, no patients to consider.

Totally alone.

'Coffee?' she asked, making a beeline for the kitchen.

'Later,' Lewis said, snagging her arm before she could go any further.

Mikki felt the drumbeat of her heart as he tugged her up against him; his eyes meshing with hers in a beat of silence that hummed with erotic promise. She sent her tongue out to moisten her mouth, desire coiling and flexing in her belly as he moved that little bit closer. 'Lewis…' Her voice sounded like it had been dragged across a rough surface. 'Should we be doing this?'

'Probably not,' he said, looking down at her mouth, the dark fan of his lashes shielding half of his eyes.

Mikki swallowed nervously. 'Maybe we should step back and be sensible about this.'

'I don't know about you but I'm not feeling too sensible right now,' he said, tipping up her chin.

She looked into those sky-blue eyes and felt another coil of desire twist a little tighter inside her. 'We're not involved any more.'

'Don't remind me.' He nipped at her bottom lip with his teeth in a soft, teasing manner.

Electric shocks ricocheted through her at the playful caress. Her lips buzzed and fizzed and fretted for more. She felt his hands settle on her hips, holding her against his stirring body, the hard presence of his need a heady reminder of where this could lead, and, even more disturbingly, how much she wanted it to.

Lewis stroked his tongue over her bottom lip, a sensual, slow brushstroke that sent another wave of longing to her toes and back. She gave a little sigh of surrender as his mouth came down and covered hers in a kiss that was as hot as fire. His tongue didn't seek entry—it took it, tangling with hers in a daring dance that was irresistibly sexy. Heat exploded inside her, the feminine dew of her body anointing her intimately as he deepened the kiss. His mouth was urgent on hers, demanding everything from her, leaving no part of her immune to his touch.

One of his hands slid from her hips to gently cup the curve of her breast, the slip and slide of satin against her flesh increasing the intoxicating allure of his caress. It was exquisite torture to be touched like this when all she wanted was to feel his hands on her, skin on skin. She pressed herself closer to him, seeking his hardness, wanting more—aching for his possession like she had never ached before. It was a fever; it was a rampant need that refused to die down. It raged through her, making her cling to him shamelessly, her mouth feeding as hungrily off his as his was off hers, her hands exploring him with urgent intent.

She worked at his bow-tie, undoing it with fingers that fumbled and fluttered in excitement. She undid the buttons of his dress shirt, sliding her palms over his chest as more and more of it was revealed. He had always been a little on the lean side, but now he had well-formed muscles that bunched under her touch. She brushed her fingertips over his flat nipples before going lower to the ridged muscles of his abdomen. She felt him quiver as she came to the waistband of his trousers and she brazenly dipped her fingers beneath it to find the hot, hard heat of him.

He was satin-wrapped steel, engorged with need, his breathing signalling how much she was affecting him. She continued to caress him, but this time she used her other hand to free him from his trousers.

'Wait,' he said, pulling her hands up to either side of her head as he brought his mouth back down heavily on hers.

There was something deeply primal about the way he was holding her, locking her in place, keeping her right where he wanted her as his mouth worked hers into a frenzy of clawing want. She arched her spine so she could feel his arousal against the quivering pulsing heart of her, relishing the way he groaned deep at the back of his throat as her tongue entwined with his.

'God, I can't believe how much I want this,' he said,

sliding his mouth down to the beating pulse at the base of her neck.

Mikki leaned her head to one side as he suckled on her sensitive skin, his teeth gently biting her, making her insides implode with longing so intense she whimpered. 'I want it too…' *Oh, dear God, how much I want it. I want you, only you!*

He dragged down the strapless top of her gown, uncovering her breasts, his eyes feasting on them for a throbbing moment before he lowered his mouth to take possession of her right nipple. She felt the hot swirl of his tongue, the intense heat like a flame licking along her taut flesh, burning, searing, branding. His teeth closed over the tight bud, and then pulled gently in a tug and release caress that made zigzags of lightning shoot up and down her spine. He moved to her other nipple, subjecting it to the same sensual assault, leaving her breathless and gasping.

'You're so beautiful,' he murmured as he eased her dress down further.

Mikki felt an errant thought slip into her mind. How many beautiful women had he had since they'd parted? She knew he would not have been celibate once she had ended their relationship. Had he been in love with anyone?

Lewis raised his head and looked at her. 'What's going on?'

Mikki bit the inside of her kiss-swollen mouth. 'I'm sorry—I can't do this…'

He held her gaze for timeless seconds. 'Too soon?'

She gave a little nod. 'I'm sorry for giving you the wrong impression.'

He let out a deep breath and stepped back from her, dragging one of his hands through his hair. 'No, don't apologise. You're probably right. It is too soon.'

She lowered her gaze, feeling a hot flush of colour rise in her cheeks. 'I'm sorry, Lewis, it's just I'm not the sleep-around sort. I don't do casual sex just for the heck of it.'

'Would it have been casual sex between us?'

She had to look at him then to try and gauge his expression, not that it gave anything away It was like trying to read a closed book. 'You know it would have been,' she said.

His eyes studied her for a long moment. 'Maybe,' he said at last. He did up the buttons of his shirt and tucked it back into his trousers. 'I'll take a rain-check on that coffee. I'll see myself out.'

'Lewis?' She hadn't been able to get her voice to work until he was almost out the front door.

He turned and looked at her. 'You made the right decision, Mikki.'

I'm not so sure about that, Mikki thought once he had left. But then she wondered what decision he had been referring to.

CHAPTER SIX

'AND to think you never said a word!' Jane was still harping on about the news that was doing the rounds of the hospital.

'That's because it's no one's business,' Mikki said, shuffling the papers on the desk.

'Oh, come on, Mikki,' Jane said. 'We've been working together for the last four years. I thought we were friends as well as colleagues.'

'I'm sorry, Jane, but I didn't say anything because I try not to think too much about that time of my life.'

Jane sat on the corner of the desk. 'What happened? What broke you guys up?'

Mikki let out a sigh and dropped her hands into her lap, her gaze going to her left hand where so briefly an engagement ring had resided. 'I was young and out of my depth and I didn't stop to think of where it would all end.'

'Sounds to me it's ended full circle,' Jane said. 'Kate was downstairs, getting something from her car, when she saw you guys dancing on the balcony on Saturday night. She said it was the most romantic thing she ever saw. So does this mean Lewis wants you back in his life?'

Mikki gave her a cheerless glance. 'I don't think so. Not permanently, in any case.'

'How can you be so sure?' Jane asked.

'Because Lewis isn't the falling–in-love type and I won't settle for anything else this time around,' she said. 'I wasted too many years of my life as it is. I want to settle down. I want to have a family. I want to be loved and love in return.'

'We all want that, Mikki,' Jane said. 'Or at least most women do. But are you sure you really know what Lewis wants now? He might have changed. People do, you know.'

'Some people do, but not Lewis,' Mikki said, although she wondered if she was being fair given how he had reacted to having discovered a half-sister. He had moved from across the globe to be near her. For someone who seemed incapable of emotion he certainly felt deep affection for Abby.

'Do you still love him?' Jane asked.

Mikki looked out at the ward through the glass partition. Patients were being attended to by nurses and some relatives were sitting by their loved ones' beds. She thought about what she had once felt for Lewis. It was not unlike the devotion Mark Upton demonstrated by being by his wife's beside all weekend.

Or was it?

Had she sat hour after hour, day after day, living in the hope that Lewis would become both physically and emotionally available to her? No, she had left on the first plane she could because she hadn't been able to face the fact that he might not have ever cared for her. She hadn't fought for their relationship. She had been too young and caught up in the romance of it all to realise she had become involved with a man, not a fantasy. Why hadn't she taken the time to get to know him instead of rushing off in a temper because he hadn't done things the way she had expected him to?

'I guess you do,' Jane said.

Mikki stood up and went to the windows overlooking the hospital car park. 'I'm not sure what I feel, to tell you the truth,' she said. 'I don't want to make the same mistakes of the past by rushing into anything I might regret.'

'Can you at least be friends?' Jane asked. 'Not all ex-couples end up enemies. Look at your parents. You're always saying how amazingly friendly they are towards each other.'

Mikki turned round. 'My parents have known each other for most of their lives. They started as friends and married as friends and divorced as friends. I admire them both for how they've conducted themselves. But I can't see myself as just a friend of Lewis's, watching him get on with his life as if we never had that time together.'

'I think you need to get him out of your system one way or the other,' Jane said. 'Maybe a little ex-sex would settle it for you.'

Mikki felt a flush creep up from her neck. 'I'm not sure that's such a great idea.'

Jane's eyes twinkled. 'Why do I get the feeling you've come close to doing exactly that?'

Mikki sent her a quelling glance as she made for the door. 'I do have some measure of self-control.'

Jane lifted her brows as she watched her leave. 'Yes, but for how long?' she asked.

Mikki had just finished changing a patient's central line when Lewis came into the unit. He was dressed in suit trousers and a shirt and tie, having spent the day consulting in his rooms on another floor of the hospital. His eyes met hers, knocking the breath right out of her body as she thought of how it had felt last night to have his mouth on hers.

'Hi,' he said. 'Have you a moment to talk through some of tomorrow's patients?'

'Sure,' she said. 'I'll meet you in the office. I just have to look at what's coming out of a patient's drain.'

When Mikki came into the office a couple of minutes later Lewis was writing up some patient notes. He looked up when she came in and rose to his feet. 'How has your day been?' he asked.

She rolled her eyes wearily. 'Long.'

'Yeah, mine too,' he said. 'On top of seeing patients I've been fielding questions about you all day from most of the staff.'

'Yes, well, I did warn you about creating a scene the other night at the ball,' Mikki said, flashing him a reproachful glance from beneath her lashes.

'They were going to find out sooner or later, Mikki.'

She chewed at her lip. 'Maybe.'

He looked at her for a pulsing moment. 'I've been doing some thinking over the weekend,' he said. 'I probably shouldn't have mentioned your father's pay-off attempt. I don't want to cause trouble between you and him. I don't hold it against him. He was just being a concerned father. He could see we were mismatched as soon as he came over to London.'

Mismatched.

Is that how he saw them, Mikki wondered. *Did he still think that?* 'It was an insulting thing to do and totally inappropriate,' she said. 'He had no right to judge you when he didn't even know you.'

'We didn't even know each other, Mikki,' he said. 'I'm starting to realise that now. I should have told you about my stuff, my baggage. It was wrong not to.'

'Then why didn't you?' she asked.

He looked at her for a beat or two. 'I wanted to, many times. I wanted to tell you about Liam and how his death changed everything. But I always felt it would have made you feel sorry for me, that you might have stuck with me out of pity, not genuine love.'

'Then you didn't know me any better than I knew you,' she replied.

He gave her one of his rare half-smiles. 'Yeah, you're probably right.'

'I just wish I hadn't had to find out about everything from Abby,' Mikki said. 'I would have preferred to hear it from you. Were you ever going to tell me about Liam?'

'I was going to tell you,' he said, 'and sooner rather than later. I felt I owed it to you, but then Abby got in first. I'm sorry about that. She was only trying to make things easier for me. She knows how painful I find it to talk about my brother.'

A little silence slipped past.

'I feel so embarrassed about my father's actions,'

Mikki said. 'You must have felt so…so angry, and rightly so.'

'I guess your father knew you wouldn't be happy with me in the long run,' he said, leaning back in his chair to look at her. 'Background issues aside, my career was always going to swamp yours.'

Mikki wondered what he would say if she were to tell him how her career had taken a back seat just lately to some of her other dreams and aspirations How she longed for much more than money in the bank and the respect and admiration of her colleagues. How she longed for someone to hold her and tell her they adored her, that they would do anything to make her happy and contented, for someone to share their deepest heart with her, their hopes and fears and dreams.

Lewis's phone broke the silence and he answered it, frowning as he listened to one of the A and E doctors relay some information. Mikki could hear the exchange and wondered if Lewis would see midnight at home or at the hospital. He closed the phone and gave her a rueful movement of his lips. 'Looks like I might have to go back to Theatre for a head injury—compound skull fracture.'

'Are you on call?' she asked.

'No, but it sounds like an acute subdural,' he said. 'By the time they get someone in, it won't be worth doing. I'm here so I may as well get on with it. Hopefully someone will return the favour some time.'

A figure appeared at the door not long after Lewis had left. Mikki turned to see John Bramley, the most senior surgeon, come in. He was frowning over the top of his bifocals. The bifocals and bushy white eyebrows gave him an intimidating air but he was anything but. He was a grandfatherly type and a great mentor of younger doctors. He was endlessly patient with both patients and relatives, caring and respectful of their wishes. She really liked working with him and had learned a lot about the difficult decisions surgeons had to make at times.

'Mikki, what's your feeling on Mrs Yates?' he asked. 'I've just spoken to the son but I don't think he realises how pointless it is to press on.'

'She's not doing well, John,' Mikki said. 'She's septic, in multi-system organ failure, on dialysis, PEEP, ino-tropes, and at this stage I have to agree with you that this is an unsalvageable situation. Even if we could somehow pull her through, her duration of survival must be short and its quality hopeless.'

'I'll have another word with the family,' he said, blowing out a tired sigh. He wrote up some notes, then turned to Mikki again, giving her a twinkling smile. 'So what's this I hear about you giving priority to your fiancé's patients in ICU?'

Mikki straightened her shoulders. 'Mr Beck is no longer my fiancé, John. And you should know me well enough to know that any decision I make about patients and their care has nothing to do with anything other than my professional judgement.'

He patted her on the shoulder. 'Only teasing, my dear,' he said. 'I know you wouldn't allow your personal issues to interfere with patient care.'

'Sorry.' She bit her lip.

He gave her a concerned frown. 'Is everything all right between you and him?'

Mikki's shoulders went down. 'It's…difficult…'

'It would be,' he said. 'But he seems a nice chap. Very well regarded in neurosurgery. Maybe this time around you can be friends.'

She gave him a wistful smile. 'I'm working on it.'

He gave her shoulder a gentle squeeze this time. 'You do that, my dear.'

Mikki watched him amble away, stopping to chat to another patient's relatives further down the corridor. She sighed as she thought about him retiring soon. It wouldn't be the same around here without him.

Kylie came in a moment later, her cheeks red hot. 'I can't believe how rude Mr Yates was to me just then,' she said, clearly close to tears but fighting it stalwartly.

Mikki gave the young woman a gentle squeeze on the elbow. 'Don't take it personally,' she said. 'He's worried about his mother.'

'But she's eighty-seven years old. She's got to die some time.'

'I know, but grief doesn't really have a use-by date,' Mikki said. 'Everyone deals with it in their own way. Mr Yates is having trouble coming to terms with things.'

'Jane mentioned something about Mrs Yates's will being changed recently,' Kylie said. 'Do you think there's something fishy going on?'

'It's complicated but I think it's just a family being a family,' Mikki said. 'Everyone is at a different stage of acceptance. I've tried to be realistic with each of them but the son does seem to be taking it the hardest.'

'Mothers and sons,' Kylie said with a knowing sigh.

One of the nurses came in with a worried look on her face. 'Dr Landon? I think you'd better call Mr Beck,' she said. 'Mrs Upton's pulse rate and blood pressure are up.'

'Call the neurosurgical theatre,' Mikki said. 'Get them to tell Mr Beck to get up here as soon as he can.' She quickly turned to Kylie. 'You'd better get CT on standby,' she said. 'We'll probably have to transfer her.'

'Right,' Kylie said, and reached for the phone.

Mikki went to the patient's bedside and checked the machines recording her status. Jenny's intracranial pressure had suddenly risen and her pulse rate and blood pressure were indeed up. All signs of a re-bleed from her recently clipped aneurysm.

'What's wrong?' Mark Upton asked with a worried look on his already ashen face.

'Try not to panic, Mark,' Mikki said. 'Mr Beck is on his way.'

Mark stood up and clutched at his wife's pale, lifeless-looking hand. 'She can't die now, Dr Landon,' he said, his throat going up and down as he tried to keep the emotion back. 'She just can't. Mr Beck was so confident. He said she would make it through this. He told us to keep positive.'

Mikki understood how neurosurgeons nearly always gave hope to patients and their families, even if it was at times rather slim. She understood how hard it was after spending hours performing difficult and stressful operations only to offer little or no hope to the relatives. Of course everyone wanted to feel positive about outcomes. It was human nature. Every neurosurgeon she had worked under adopted the same approach: it's not over until it's over. But Mikki saw all too often the other side of it: patients who suffered a stroke or multiple strokes after invasive surgery. Offering hope when there was none seemed wrong to her. She felt it was better for loved ones to be prepared for the worst, even if it didn't happen. That was much better than getting their hopes up, only to have to smash them when things went wrong.

Mikki saw Lewis enter the unit and turned back to Mark. 'Maybe you should go and get a coffee while we see to Jenny,' she said. 'We'll send someone to get you if there's any change.'

Mark let go of his wife's hand. 'Don't let her die, please.'

Lewis by this time had reached them, and added his reassurances. 'Do as Dr Landon says, Mark, we'll let you know what's going on as soon as possible.'

'What's her ICP doing, Mikki?' Lewis asked, turning to Mikki.

Mikki was busy hand-delivering a bolus of mannitol into Jenny's central line. 'It jumped to twelve about fifteen minutes ago. She's had a bolus of prednisolone and I'm just getting mannitol on board. What do you want to do?'

'We need to CT her now,' Lewis said. 'She's probably had a bleed at the clip, but we have to be sure before we open again. Either way, this is bad. Unless we do something soon, we'll lose her.' He pushed out a sigh of frustration. 'I suppose CT will be half an hour getting here.'

'CT is here now,' she said, glancing across at the transfer team. 'I got Kylie to call them while the nurse called you from Theatre.'

'Good work, Mikki,' he said. 'That was a damn good move on your part.'

She gave him a stiff movement of her lips and turned back to the patient to assist the transfer team. 'We'll let you know what we find. Keep your phone on.'

Forty minutes later Lewis answered his phone in the theatre change room. 'Lewis Beck.'

'It's Mikki. The scans are through,' she said. 'There's been a bleed but it's tiny. Most of the pressure is oedema. The radiologist has called in Peter Craven to have a look. He's the radiology head and the main interventionalist here. He's here now, looking at the films. They think it's amenable to coiling.'

'Great,' Lewis said, scraping his hand through his hair. 'That'd be better than wading through oedematous brain. I'm on my way down. I had to give the registrar a hand back in theatre.'

By the time Lewis arrived in Radiology the final films were on the monitor, being pored over by Peter Craven while Mikki was supervising the transfer of the patient back onto the ICU bed.

Lewis watched as Mikki carefully positioned Jenny on the bed, as if she was not just a patient but a close and much-treasured friend. He had switched his feelings off as soon as he had diagnosed Jennifer Upton. Yes, it mattered that she was a young mum and her husband was frantic with worry, but Lewis had cleared his mind of all of that in order to maintain a clinical distance. But

Mikki was able to somehow do both. She was efficient and professional at all times and yet she brought something extra to the patients and their loved ones. Since the news of their past history had been doing the rounds of the hospital he had heard nothing but praise about his ex-fiancée. Her dedication, her focus and self-sacrificing attitude was held in high esteem from the top level of management to the cleaning staff. One of the ladies from the kitchen, when she had restocked the theatre staffroom fridge, had even questioned why Lewis had let her go.

He had mumbled something noncommittal in reply but ever since he had been back in Australia he had been asking himself the very same question. Was that why he had taken the job? He hadn't thought so at the time but there was no underestimating the subconscious. Look at how he had snapped up that house across from Mikki's. It was ridiculously overpriced but he had bought it anyway. He'd wanted to be near her. Was that weird? Was that leaning towards stalking? No, it was more about trying to sort out the detritus of the past. He had not handled things well. He had not done the things he should have done. He had let her go and he had lived to regret it.

A voice brought him out of his momentary reverie. 'Hello, I assume you're the new neurosurgeon, Lewis Beck?'

'Yes, that's right,' Lewis said offering a hand to the radiologist.

'I'm Peter Craven, Radiology. I do most of the vascular interventional radiology. It's good to have you on board.' He pointed to the scans on the monitor in front of him. 'Nice work.'

'This was more of an AV malformation than an aneurysm,' Lewis explained. 'It was very hard to preserve the main outflow, but clipping it was the best option.'

'I don't know how you got that clip on there—it looks like an anatomical impossibility to me. Anyway, there's a tiny leak from the inflow side. That bit I could get at and use gel and not block outflow. There's a lot of oedema around so more surgery would be pretty destructive, I imagine.'

'It would for sure,' Lewis said. 'What do you want to do, then?'

'Mikki has agreed to stay put in Radiology and supervise her support while I do the procedure. That will make things a lot more comfortable for Radiology,' Peter said.

'Yes, everything's under control upstairs with the registrar, and Bashir Ahmed is coming on duty in half an hour,' Mikki said from across the room. 'He'll have to get the handover from the registrar. I'm happy to stay here till we're through.'

'Thanks, Mikki,' Lewis said. 'Jenny Upton's fluid control and oxygenation are going to be absolutely critical here.'

'You should get home,' she said. 'You've been operating for over twelve hours.'

'It was thirteen and a half at last count,' Lewis said, rubbing the back of his aching neck. 'I'll go and have a word with the husband.'

'I called him as soon as Peter identified the problem,' Mikki said. 'He promised to go home and get some sleep once Jenny's back in the unit. You should do the same.'

Lewis gave her an ironic look. 'And how long have you been on duty?'

'Long enough to have lost count,' she said, and turned back to the patient.

CHAPTER SEVEN

MIKKI was just getting into her car when a shadow appeared at her open driver's door and her heart nearly jumped right out of her chest. She clutched at her throat, her breathing so ragged she couldn't get her voice to work for a moment or two.

'Sorry, did I scare you?' Lewis said.

'I—I thought you had left hours ago,' she said.

'I did some paperwork in my rooms,' he said. 'It hardly seemed fair to go home to bed while you were still here looking after my patient.'

'It's my job,' she said, looking at the dashboard rather than his ice-floe eyes.

'Maybe, but you don't have to go the extra mile for me.'

'I wasn't doing it for you,' she said. 'I was doing it for Jenny Upton.'

'All the same, I appreciate it.'

Mikki tucked a loose strand of hair back behind her ear with a hand that wasn't quite steady. 'I'd better be going…' She forced herself to meet his eyes. 'Was there something in particular you wanted to see me about?'

'Actually, I was wondering if you could give me a lift.'

She frowned at him. 'What happened to your car?'

'It had to go back to the workshop,' he said. 'There was a problem with the fuel-injection system. I didn't get a chance to pick it up as I was stuck in Theatre for so long.'

'There's a taxi rank at the front of the hospital,' she said, hating herself for sounding so uncharitable and unhelpful but it was late and she was tired and she was too affected by his presence to trust herself with him even for the short duration of a car trip. She could still taste his kiss. Every time she licked her lips she felt the tingles of where he had been. Every nerve was affected, hungry for more. He would only have to look at her mouth and she would be tempted to press hers to his. And who knew what would happen next? Well, she did know and that's why she needed some distance.

'There's a fifteen-minute waiting time,' Lewis said. 'I already checked. Apparently there's a concert on at the entertainment centre tonight.'

Mikki triggered the passenger door lock as she let out a sigh of defeat. 'Get in.'

He got in and gave her directions to the serviced apartment he was renting in Bondi, and after a lengthy period of silence asked, 'What's wrong, Mikki?'

'Nothing.'

He gave a short bark of wry laughter. 'When a woman says nothing is wrong it invariably means the opposite. What have I done now?'

'You haven't done anything,' she said. 'I'm just tired.' *And I think I'm falling in love with you all over again.*

'Yes, it's been one of those days, that's for sure,'

he said. 'It was a bad moment when I got that call from ICU.'

Mikki flicked her gaze to him as she waited for a traffic light to change. 'Mark Upton was beside himself with panic,' she said. She faced the road again and added, 'He didn't seem prepared at all for something like this happening. I don't think it's wise to give people such hope when nothing is certain in this game.'

'I don't believe in shattering people's hopes just to keep my back covered if something goes wrong,' he said. 'I know there are risks and not everyone makes it, but I don't want people to think I am not confident in my own ability to turn things around.'

'Jennifer Upton still might not make it,' Mikki said.

'I hope you didn't say that to her husband.'

Again she felt his gaze on her, but hard this time, like blocks of ice. 'I tried to be realistic,' Mikki said. 'People don't take everything in when they're being spoken to by their specialist. They get flooded with emotion and fear and panic. I see it as my job to help them face reality. To get some sort of balance on things, to prepare them for the worst.'

'That seems rather pessimistic to me,' he said. 'But, then, given what happened between us, I guess it's pretty true to character.'

Mikki's gaze darted to his again. 'What do you mean by that?'

His expression was carved from marble, hard, impenetrable, unyielding. 'You always believed the worst of me. I wasn't there for you. I always put my career first. I didn't understand how you felt about losing the baby. I didn't love you the way you wanted to be loved. I didn't give enough in our relationship. Have I missed anything?'

Mikki's hands gripped the wheel so tightly her fingers hurt. 'Are we talking here about the relationship that would never have lasted as long as it did if I hadn't fallen pregnant?'

'You didn't even ask me why I wasn't there to support you when you lost the baby,' he said tightly. 'Do you realise that? You never asked. You just assumed.'

Mikki opened her mouth but just as quickly closed it. He was looking at her with anger and frustration, and hurt was in there somewhere too. It was a shock to her to be confronted with her own failings. Failings she had not recognised in herself before.

'I was stuck in Theatre with a difficult case,' he went on. 'I was working with a particularly demanding consultant. He wouldn't allow personal issues to compromise the patient under his care. I agreed with him but can you imagine how torn I felt? I wanted to be there for you but how could I? The patient on the table had to be the priority. The irony is they ended up dying after three and a half hours in Theatre. I lost out on both counts.'

Mikki finally found her voice but it was barely audible. 'I wish you had told me. I would have understood.'

'How could I tell you anything?' he asked. 'You were glaring at me as soon as I walked in the door, making me feel like the worst person in the world. I decided to take it on the chin. You were upset enough without another showdown. I thought we'd sort it out later.'

'But we never did…'

She heard him shift in his seat, the leather protesting at the movement. 'No, we never did.'

Mikki looked at the road ahead but she was aware of Lewis's gaze on her. 'I never felt convinced you were totally committed to having a family. I felt like I had completely ruined your career plans.'

'I admit marriage and a family wasn't at the top of my lists of things to do back then,' he said. 'But as I've got older I've seen how a good relationship could add a dimension to one's life that living alone doesn't.'

A pain that felt like a stab wound assailed Mikki at his words. Did he have someone in mind? Was he actively searching for someone to take over where she had left off? 'What about kids?' she asked, keeping her eyes trained on the road ahead. 'Do you want a family of your own someday?'

It seemed a second or two, maybe longer before he answered. 'Do you?'

'I asked you first,' Mikki said, unconsciously holding her breath.

The leather squeaked again as he moved. 'I'd be lying if I said I didn't think about it now and again. I think that's how my time in Afghanistan changed me. I thought about my mortality. You forget about it when you're the one saving other people's lives. That's why doctors make such terrible patients. They never think they will get ill like everyone else. But out there I realised that when I die there will be no one to carry on after me. It's a sobering thought.'

Mikki kept silent. She felt that pain again, deep and biting. If her pregnancy hadn't ended in a miscarriage they would have had a six-year-old child by now. He or she might have had a brother or sister to complete their family unit. She tried not to think of their little faces, their dark hair and blue or brown eyes and lean, healthy limbs. She tried not to think of what his future children with someone else would look like but the images taunted her all the same. How would she deal with it if he came into the hospital one day in the not-too-distant future to announce his engagement, let alone the birth of a child? She would have to smile and congratulate him just like everyone else. She would have to pretend to be happy for him while inside she was torn apart with grief at what they could have had together if only things hadn't gone the way they had. How did her mother do it? How could she be *pleased* about her ex-husband marrying his young girlfriend Rebecca and having a second family with her?

'How about you?' Lewis asked.

Mikki lifted one shoulder up and down, desperate to disguise her spiralling emotions. 'It's hard to have a career and kids, especially in medical specialties with the long hours and on-call demands. Getting the balance right is hard. I see so many women trying to have it all only to end up stressed and feeling guilty that they're not doing anything right.'

'You didn't really answer my question.'

'That's because it's none of your business.' She flashed him a quick glance and added, 'Any more.'

His top lip curled sardonically. 'You really like to drive that point home, don't you, sweetheart?'

Mikki's knuckles went white on the steering-wheel. 'I told you not to call me that.'

'My apartment is in the next street on the left,' he said ignoring her reprimand.

Mikki parked out the front of his apartment block and kept the engine running, her fingers drumming impatiently on the steering-wheel, her eyes staring straight ahead.

'Do you fancy a nightcap or something?' he asked.

'No, thank you,' she said in a clipped tone.

One of his hands reached out and stroked the nape of her neck, the warm caress melting her tight ligaments, turning her stiff bones into warmed-up wax. 'I'm sorry, Mikki,' he said. 'I'm not handling this well, am I? I don't want us to argue all the time. Can we just have a cup of coffee together and let the past go for a bit?'

Mikki's stomach did a dip and dive as his fingers captured her chin to turn her head to face him. Suddenly the thought of going home to her empty town house wasn't so attractive. The thought of company for half an hour or so over a coffee or cup of tea was tempting, far too tempting to resist. 'Just one coffee,' she said. 'But only because I want to check out the view from your apartment.'

He gave her one of his rare smiles. 'Then let's go and check it out.'

It was superb, Mikki thought as she looked out from the windows a short time later. The sea was rolling in on waves that crashed against the shore with thunderous pounding, before being sucked back with the strong winter undertow.

'What do you think?' Lewis asked as he came over with cups and teaspoons and placed them on a coffee table next to the sofa.

'It's great,' Mikki said. 'Do you have nice views from your place across from mine?'

'Yes, it's one of the reasons I bought it.'

'It's a big house for one person,' Mikki said as he went back for the coffee.

'I like my space,' he said as he came back. 'Remember the tiny flat I had in London?'

Mikki felt a pang as the small, cramped residence came to mind. Some of her happiest and saddest times had been spent there. 'Yes.'

'I moved out a couple of months after you left,' he said. 'I bought a three-storey place in Mayfair. It was hard, keeping up the mortgage payments, but I really enjoyed having the space to put things where I wanted them without feeling crowded.'

'What a pity I didn't stay a little longer,' she said dryly. 'A house in Mayfair would have really impressed my father.'

He gave her a direct look. 'Do you ever do anything without thinking of whether or not your mother or father would approve or disapprove?'

Mikki folded her arms across her body. 'I'm almost thirty years old,' she said. 'Of course I don't need their approval.'

He came over to where she was standing. 'Are you going to tell your mother we kissed the other night?'

She tried to back away but there was nowhere to go. 'No.'

His mouth slanted in a half-smile. 'Why not?'

'Because it's none of her business.'

He moved even closer, close enough to touch, close enough for her to feel the warmth of his body, close enough for her to feel the magnetic pull of his gaze as it held hers. 'You won't tell her because deep down you're worried she'll encourage you to give our relationship another go,' he said. 'She thinks you should take me back on whatever terms I'm prepared to offer.'

Mikki's eyes became round. 'Has she said something to that effect to you?'

'I ran into her when I was in the city, picking up something for Abby. Your mother is concerned about you,' he said. 'She thinks you don't get out enough. She thinks you work too hard and neglect other areas of your life.'

She clenched her teeth. 'I can't believe I'm hearing this. My divorced mother is trying to set me up with my ex-fiancé, the man she and my father thought was totally wrong for me seven years ago. What sort of farce is this?'

His brows rose ever so slightly. 'You're not tempted to see where this takes us?' he asked.

Mikki was not only tempted, she could barely think about anything else. Seeing him again, not to mention the heated kiss they had exchanged, had made it all the more apparent she wasn't over him. She had been so sure she could handle working alongside him, but it was impossible to put their past to one side. It kept rising up like a spectre to haunt her. The way they had got together, the way they had broken up, the way it had all happened so quickly that she hadn't spent the amount of time she should have thinking about how to handle the difficulties they had faced. If she had learned anything over the last seven years, it was she had to put the brakes on, to make sure each action she took wasn't going to be one she regretted later. She raised her chin but it wasn't quite the show of defiance she wanted to pull off. 'I came in for coffee. I didn't sign up for anything else.'

'Yeah, I remember,' he said, looking at her mouth. 'You think it's too soon, but I think the sooner we do this the better for both of us.'

Mikki moistened her lips with the tip of her tongue, her heart hammering like a piston, her resolve already taking a tumble. 'Lewis...'

He cupped her face in his large hands, his thumbs moving in a slow caress on her cheeks, his eyes—those incredibly blue eyes—locked on hers. 'Why fight what's inevitable?' he asked.

She swallowed the knot of panic in her throat. 'We hate each other,' she said. 'We're strangers now. We have nothing in common. We—'

He blocked the rest of her paltry excuses with the pad of his thumb. 'I don't hate you, Mikki,' he said. 'I've never hated you.'

Mikki felt her breath trip over something thorn-like in the middle of her chest. She couldn't speak for the emotion welling up inside her.

Lewis gave her a rueful look as he went back to stroking her cheeks with his thumbs. 'I admit I was angry with you, crazily, scarily angry. I couldn't believe you would just walk away like that. But then I felt relieved. I figured it was for the best. You would get back to your life, the perfect life your parents had planned for you: a well-established career; marriage to a nice man from a good background some time in the future; the two point two kids. I had to let you go. It seemed the right thing to do.'

Mikki moistened her lips. 'You didn't ask me to come back. You didn't even call me.'

His hands dropped from her face as he stepped back from her. 'No,' he said, moving a few feet away. 'I didn't.'

'Doesn't that say something to you about the futility of any relationship between us?' she asked.

He turned and looked at her again. 'Back then, yes, but now it's different.'

Mikki felt her heart kick again as his eyes meshed with hers. 'You're not suggesting we try again...are you?'

He returned to her, taking her hands in his, holding them against his chest. 'I'm not suggesting another go at anything permanent at this stage,' he said. 'I think that would be repeating the mistake we made before by rushing in before we've had time to think things through. But I do think neither of us will truly move on until we get some form of closure.'

'Closure?' she said, frowning as she pulled her hands out of his hold. 'You want to sleep with me just to get some closure on our past? Is that what you're saying?'

'Why do you always twist my words?' he asked, frowning back at her. 'I want to sleep with you because I damn well want you like an ache in my gut.'

His blunt admission rang in the silence that ensued, filling the air with echoes of eroticism.

Mikki cautiously sent her tongue out over her lips again. 'You seem fairly confident I want the same thing.'

'Deny it if you feel the need to,' he said. 'But I bet

if I kissed you right now I would have all the proof I need.'

Mikki raised her chin in a last show of truculence. She knew she was beaten. She suspected he knew it too, but she was damned if she was going to go down without at least some of her pride intact. 'You'd dare to do that?'

He gave a ghost of a smile that was devastatingly attractive. 'Yeah,' he said, taking her by the shoulders and pulling her up against him. 'You're right, I would.' And then his mouth closed over hers.

There was a little voice inside Mikki's head that tried to tell her to stop this before it went any further, but the gentle but firm pressure of his lips on hers had an intoxicating effect, leaving her at the mercy of her reawakened senses. She sighed as she gave herself up to the tender assault on her mouth, her lips swelling as the pressure subtly increased. She opened at the first commanding stroke of his tongue, melting inside and out as he explored her mouth in intimate, erotic detail, calling her tongue into a slow, sensual waltz that within minutes became a fast-paced tango.

Need burst through the pores of her skin as he pulled her closer, his arms like tight bands as they held her to him. She felt the rush of his blood to his groin, the response that was such a breathtaking reminder of how quickly he became aroused and how she was swept away by the potent power of it. It was like a moving force in her body—urgent, insistent, pleading for assuagement. The sensual movements of his tongue inside the moist, warm cave of her mouth were a sexy mimic of how his strong male body could have the same devastatingly delicious effect on her feminine core, probing, thrusting and then withdrawing, only to claim her all over again. Her body quivered with the past memory of it, longing for it to happen all over again. She wanted the earth-shattering lift-off, the release from all thought and reason that was as euphoric as any strong drug.

Lewis's mouth moved from hers to the sensitive skin of her neck, his lips nibbling and his tongue stroking her into a frenzy of want that was overwhelming. She whimpered with longing as one of his hands cupped her breast in a gentle but possessive caress that sent a shower of sparks down her spine. She felt the tight nub of her nipple pressing into his palm, the intense ache for more of his touch like a fever rampaging in her blood. She pressed herself against him, the instinctive plea for him to satiate this aching burning need overpowering any common sense she had fooled herself she had once possessed.

His mouth went back to her mouth, imprinting her lips with the possessive urgency of his. His tongue flicked against hers, calling her back into another dance of mutual desire. She partnered it with hers, coiling, darting, stroking, slipping away, only to come back for more.

Lewis turned her in his arms, lifting her in one strong movement that sent the breath out of her lungs as he carried her to his bedroom, his mouth still locked on hers as if he couldn't bear to break the intimate contact just yet.

Mikki wrapped her arms about his neck, breathing in the scent of him, enjoying the magic of being in his arms, of feeling his strength and the heady potency of his kiss.

He came down with her on the mattress, his long legs trapping hers in a sexy embrace that left her in no doubt of his urgent need. She felt it throbbing against her feminine mound, the heavy pulse of his blood ricocheting throughout her body.

His hands began to work on her clothes, slowly at first but then with increasing urgency as the momentum of passion increased. Mikki's fingers fumbled with his shirt buttons in her haste to get them undone so she could plant hot, moist kisses to the muscled wall of his chest. She tasted the salt and musk of his skin once she had uncovered it, drawing her tongue down over his sternum, her stomach coiling with delight when she heard him make a sound of pleasure deep at the back of his throat. This was the Lewis she remembered so well. Hungry for her, his body primed for action, the hectic pace of his breathing as he fought for control. She wondered if he had ever been as hungry for other women as he was for her. She hoped not. She prayed not. This was too special, too intimate and precious to be shared, to be replicated as if it was some cheap B-grade movie instead of a timeless epic.

Mikki undid his belt and then his trousers, sliding down the zipper to claim her prize. She heard him draw in a sharp breath as her fingers danced over his tented underwear, her belly turning over at the thought of him filling her as he had done in the past.

He sucked in another breath as she peeled back his underwear. She stroked him, slowly at first, a gentle,

worshipful exploration of his maleness, her senses filling
with the scent of his arousal.

'You're driving me insane, Mikki,' he said in a rough-
sounding burr.

'Mmm,' she said, and lowered her mouth to him in a
daring caress, swirling her tongue over and around him
until he gave another deep groan, his hands clutching
the back of her head as if he wasn't sure if he wanted
to hold her to him or push her away. She delighted in
the way his body was preparing for the final explosion
of release. She could feel the pressure building in him,
the turgidity of his length under the ministrations of her
lips and tongue making her feel powerful in an utterly
feminine way.

'That's enough,' he said, pulling away, his breathing
hard and fast-paced.

Mikki knew what was coming next as he pushed her
back down on the mattress, his weight pinning her as his
mouth covered hers in a searing kiss, hard, passionate,
urgent. She squirmed with pleasure under the hardened
probe of his flesh against hers, the delicious ache between her thighs making her mindless with need.

She wriggled out of the rest of her clothes, watching
as he shucked off the rest of his. His body was deeply
tanned, lean and strong, every muscle cut to perfec-
tion, carved and shaped by hard physical exercise. His
abdomen was a network of rippling muscle, and she
danced her fingers over the hard ridges, exploring him,
delighting in his urgent response to her.

Her skin brushed up against his hair-roughened
thighs, every nerve of hers quivering in delight. It felt
so amazing to be in his arms again, to feel the heat of his

mouth as it fed so hungrily off hers, to feel the intense longing that flared between them like an unstoppable tide.

Lewis tore his mouth from hers, his breathing hard as he looked down at her. 'I need to get a condom,' he said. 'Wait right here.' He got off the bed and went to his trousers lying on the floor, picking them up to retrieve his wallet from the back pocket.

Mikki drew in a hitching breath as he applied the protection. She was so ready for him, impatient to feel his possession after so long without the intimacy of his touch. Her skin tingled as he came back to her, his thighs nudging hers apart, his weight propped up on his elbows as he captured her mouth in another heart-stopping kiss. She felt the building urgency of his lips and tongue, the way he was fighting for control as his body sought the secret sanctuary of hers.

She gasped when he moved inside her with that first delicious thrust. It was just as exhilarating as the very first time, the feel of his body stretching her, the way his body filled her, exciting her flesh, awakening her nerves to flickering, frenzied awareness. A deep ache burned inside her, low in her belly, triggering a thousand tiny pulses in between her thighs. Tension built as he drove a little harder, as if he couldn't hold back. She arched up to meet every downward rock of his pelvis, relishing the way his possession carried her closer and closer to the edge of reason. She was nothing but feeling. Physical feeling that transcended everything she had felt before. The climb to the summit was faster than she had ever experienced before. Her senses were screaming for release, clamouring for the euphoria of being let loose in the warm, sensual sea of sexual fulfilment. The first wave of release hit her like a rolling wave, followed by another and another. She was tumbling over and over in the ripples of ecstasy, her mind empty but for the pleasure of absolute fulfilment.

Lewis took his own pleasure with a primal grunt of release that made Mikki's skin shiver in delight. He thrust deep and hard as he emptied himself, the skin of his back and shoulders peppered with fine goose-bumps under the caressing glide of her hands.

He lay slumped over her, his body heavy with lassitude, his breathing still uneven as he spoke against her neck. 'Am I too heavy for you?'

'No,' she said, running her hands over his taut buttocks.

He eased up to look at her, his body still encased in hers. 'No regrets?'

She sank her teeth in her bottom lip. 'Some, I guess...'

He brushed the hair off her face, his blue eyes darker than normal as they held hers. 'This isn't a one-night stand, Mikki,' he said.

'What is it then?' she asked.

He held her look for an endless moment, his eyes searching hers until she felt as if he could see the deepest yearnings of her heart. She tried to mask her emotions. She was supposed to hate him. She was supposed to have moved on. But being in his arms again had proved how little she had travelled from the heartbreak of their short-lived relationship.

'It can be whatever we want it to be,' Lewis said.

Mikki studied his mouth, her heart giving a little

tripping movement inside her chest when she thought of how much she had missed his kisses, his touch and his glorious, mind-blowing love-making. She brought her gaze back to his, wondering what he was thinking, what he was feeling, if anything. Men were hardwired to enjoy sex on a physical level. Emotions didn't always come into it, or at least not the same way they did for most women. 'Are you suggesting an affair of some sort?' she asked.

His mouth slanted a fraction. 'I'm not sure what one calls a relationship with one's ex-fiancée.'

'It's called a mistake,' Mikki said with a wry look. 'Sequels don't always turn out as good as the original.'

His half-smile disappeared and a frown settled between his brows. 'Why are you so determined to not even give this a chance?' he asked.

Mikki pushed against his chest and rolled out from beneath him. She grabbed the nearest article of clothing and vainly tried to cover herself.

'Mikki, come on,' he said as he too rose from the bed. 'Don't put this wall up between us.'

She turned on him. 'You think I'm the one putting up walls? What about you with your secret family? I was *engaged* to you, Lewis. You didn't tell me about your brother. You still haven't told me anything about him. I know there wasn't much time to get to know each other properly back then but surely something as important and life changing as that should have come up at some point?'

He raked a hand through his hair, his eyes moving away from hers. 'I didn't tell you about my family because it was a painful part of my past I wanted to put behind me. I got used to being alone. I preferred it that way.'

Mikki let out a breath. 'I'm not sure I can do this your way, Lewis,' she said. 'You want to get closure. I understand that, I want it too. But you're still the loner you always were. You don't want the same things I want.'

'I suppose you mean marriage and kids,' he said.

She searched his features for something, anything, but it was as blank as the wall behind him. 'I'm nearly thirty years old, Lewis. I want a family. I've always wanted that. I thought we were going to have that but then...well, it didn't work out.'

He picked up his trousers and stepped into them, before throwing his shirt on but leaving it undone. 'I didn't want this to happen,' he said, waving his hand towards the wrinkled bed where moments before they had been writhing in passion.

Mikki raised her brows sceptically. 'Oh, come on, Lewis. You expect me to believe that?'

'It's true,' he said, letting out a heavy breath. 'I came back to Australia expecting to run into you and to feel nothing. I've run into ex partners before and there's never been an issue. But with you it's different. I don't know why but it just is.'

'Maybe because I was the one who ended it,' she said. 'It's your ego we're talking about here, nothing else.'

'You think that is what this is about?' he asked. 'Mikki, we just had sex. Great sex. Brilliant sex. I want you. You want me. That's what this is about. I thought what we had was over. I wanted it to be over. I thought by coming out to this job I would prove to myself it was well and truly over.'

'It has to be over,' Mikki said. 'We've been apart for seven years.'

He came over and took her by the hands, holding her in front of him, his eyes locked on hers. 'It's not over, though, is it, Mikki?' he asked softly.

She looked into his eyes and felt her chest tighten. How could it be over when she still loved him so much? 'No, I guess not...' she said on a feather-soft sigh as his mouth came down and sealed hers.

CHAPTER EIGHT

MIKKI lay in the circle of Lewis's arms after the storm of passion had subsided. Her body was still humming with the aftershocks of the cataclysmic release she had experienced. The intensity of her response to Lewis's love-making made her realise how truly vulnerable she was. It was as if nothing had changed from all those years ago when she had been so young and innocent and trusting. She had wanted Lewis on whatever terms he'd offered then. He wouldn't have offered marriage back then if it hadn't been for her accidental pregnancy. And he certainly wasn't offering it now. He was offering an affair, a relationship that had a finite end in sight. It would be foolish to expect anything else.

'Why don't you stay the night?' Lewis asked in the silence.

Mikki turned her head on the pillow to look at him. 'I should get going. I have an early start.'

He touched her cheek with a long finger. 'Have dinner with me tomorrow.'

'Are you asking me or telling me?' she said.

He rolled back towards her, pinning her beneath him, the stirring of his body against hers making her senses go haywire all over again. 'Are you agreeing or refusing?' he countered.

How could she refuse him anything? she wondered. 'To tell you the truth, Lewis, I'm not sure what I'm doing,' she said, momentarily chewing her lip. 'This seems right but wrong at the same time. Does that make sense?'

He caressed her bottom lip with the pad of his thumb. 'I think it will sort itself out one way or the other,' he said. 'We just need some time to explore what's still between us.'

'What are we going to tell people?' Mikki asked. 'It's not as if we can hide the fact that we're seeing each other, no matter how casually. I've already had a teasing comment from John Bramley about giving priority to your patients.'

'I know how hard it is to keep things private in a hospital,' he said. 'But this is our business, no one else's.'

Mikki closed her eyes as his mouth came down over hers, his kiss long and lingering before he finally released her.

'You need to get some sleep,' he said, helping her to her feet. 'Let me drive you home in your car and pick you up in the morning.'

'No, I'm fine,' she said, slipping her feet into her shoes. 'I can make my own way home.'

'No, I want to take you home,' he said. 'I want to spend the rest of the night with you, maybe even a couple of nights. Otherwise you might accuse me of having a one-night stand with you.'

She gave him a look on her way out of his room. 'I promise not to accuse you of that.'

'Yeah, well, I'm not going to risk it,' he said, heading back to the bedroom.

She turned and followed him, watching as he collected a fresh set of clothes from the wardrobe. 'You don't have to do this, Lewis. I'm perfectly capable of going home by myself.'

He moved through to the en suite and came out with a small toiletry bag and placed it and the clothes in an overnight bag. 'You will do as you are told, Mikki,' he said, zipping up the bag.

Her eyes flared. 'You're acting like an overbearing husband.'

His eyes came back to hers as he snatched up the bag. 'I don't believe in making love with you and then letting you go home alone as if nothing has changed.'

Mikki's spine went rigid. 'You can't just take control of my life like this,' she stormed. 'Nothing has changed. We made love—no, strike that. We had sex. Ex-sex. As far as I'm concerned, nothing has changed.'

'Everything has changed, Mikki,' he said.

'How has it changed? You haven't got any claim on me now, Lewis. We are free agents. So we had sex. Big deal. It was just sex.'

'It was not just sex,' he bit out. 'You know what it was.'

'Actually, I don't. Perhaps you could fill in the gaps for me.'

'You and I have some unfinished business,' he said as he wheeled past her and out of the door.

'Now, wait just a minute,' she said, following him with angry strides.

He held the front door open for her. 'Don't fight me

on this, Mikki,' he said with an intransigent look. 'We blew it last time. Let's not do it again.'

'Hang on a minute,' Mikki said. 'Just what exactly are you saying?'

His jaw was locked like a bolt across the door of a fortress. 'I think we need to give ourselves another chance.'

She widened her eyes at him. 'Are you out of your mind?'

He jerked his head towards the exit. 'Get into the car, Mikki.'

She jabbed a finger into his chest. 'You don't get to tell me what to do and when to do it. You are nothing to me, do you hear me? Nothing.'

'So you just sleep around for the heck of it these days?' he shot back.

'I don't have to answer that.'

'You don't need to because I already know the answer,' he said. 'It's why I'm insisting on coming back to your place. I'm not going to budge on this, Mikki.'

Mikki ground her teeth and stalked past him, anger and frustration simmering inside her. She refused to speak to him on the journey to her house. She sat stiffly beside him; her gaze fixed on the road ahead, her hands in tight knots in her lap. She felt like her life was spinning out of her control. By succumbing to the temptation of being in his arms again she had been catapulted back into his life in a way she wasn't sure was wise at this point. It was too early. She hadn't had time to prepare herself, to protect herself from being hurt all over again. She was as vulnerable as ever, maybe even more so.

'You can brood and pout all you like,' Lewis said as

he turned into her street. 'But I am not leaving you until we sort out some stuff between us.'

She sent him a glowering look, her lips pressed tightly together.

'I realise me staying at your place or you at mine will give the gossipmongers something to play with, but it can't be avoided,' he went on. 'People have already been talking about us.'

Mikki could just imagine what was being said. She loathed having her private life speculated on but she couldn't see how it could be avoided now everyone knew she and Lewis had once been engaged. People always took sides and she knew whose side most people would be on. She would be cast as the deserter, the runaway bride who hadn't supported her hard-working husband in establishing his career. She had put her needs and career before his, running away at the first hurdle they'd faced. The trouble was that in hindsight Mikki felt she *was* partly to blame. She hadn't worked at getting to know Lewis better. She hadn't explored the depths to his character. If he had felt closer to her, wouldn't he have told her about his background? She had spent far too much time talking about *her* background, how she wanted some space from her controlling parents, how she wanted to prove to them she could stand on her own two feet. In her youth and inexperience she had let her issues create an imbalance in their relationship.

Lewis pulled up in her driveway and turned the engine off to look at her. 'I want us to be friends as well as lovers, Mikki. I know it's a difficult combination but I think we can do it.'

Mikki was finding her relationship with him right

here and now the thing most difficult to handle. All the boundaries had shifted. She wasn't sure what was expected of her and what to expect from him. It would not be so easy to walk away this time. She wondered how on earth she had done it before.

He closed the door and came over to her. He placed his hands on her shoulders, meshing his gaze with hers. 'Would you prefer me to use the spare bedroom to give you a little space?' he asked.

Mikki felt the warmth of his hands searing her flesh, the electric pulse of his body in contact with hers. It set her senses alight all over again, the banked-down fires of need stirring to hot, fervent life, making her body sway involuntarily towards him. His arms came around her, pulling her up against his thighs, bringing her into the tempting territory of his arousal. She didn't speak but she let her body do the talking for her. She pressed her breasts into the wall of his chest, delighting in the rush of sensations the intimate contact caused. She ran her tongue over her lips, dampening them in preparation for his already descending mouth. She closed her eyes as his lips took hers in a searing kiss, hot and full of longing, almost bruising in its urgency. She responded with everything that was in her, with all the pent-up need of the years they had spent apart, and with all the years of heartache she might have in front of her without him.

He suddenly pulled out of the kiss and gave her a rueful look. 'You know something?' he said. 'I think I will take the spare bedroom. We both have to work tomorrow and I don't want to keep you awake any longer.'

Mikki knew her disappointment was showing on her

face. 'I can assure you I've had much later nights than this,' she said.

He brushed her cheek with his fingertip. 'Yes, so have I, but the thing is…I'm out of condoms.'

'Oh…'

He tipped up her chin and kissed her mouth again, softly, briefly. 'Do you have any?' he asked.

She shook her head, feeling embarrassed, gauche and out of touch. 'No…'

He frowned as his hand fell back to his side. 'You have been practising safe sex for the last seven years, haven't you?' he asked.

She blushed even further. 'I haven't needed to…'

His frown deepened. 'I'm not sure what you're saying.'

Mikki met his gaze. 'Lewis, I haven't been having sex. Not once. I haven't even come close. There's been no one since you.'

His expression became incredulous. 'No one? No one at all?'

She shook her head. 'No one.'

'But why?' he asked, still frowning.

Mikki shrugged. 'Lack of time, lack of interest, lack of opportunity.'

He still looked confounded. 'You're not still carrying some sort of torch for me, are you?' he asked after a lengthy pause. 'I kind of figured you'd fallen out of love with me after we lost the baby.'

She turned away. 'That would really please you, wouldn't it?' she said over her shoulder. 'That after all this time I was in love with you.'

'Are you?'

Mikki forced herself to face him. 'What would be the point? You don't love me. You only ever said it once you heard about the baby. I never knew for sure if you loved me for me or for the baby.'

His eyes shifted from hers as he moved to the other side of the room, his back turned to her, his gaze on the ocean thundering against the shore outside. 'I can't give you what you want, Mikki,' he said. 'The thing is, I never could. That's why I had to let you go. I thought you'd be better off with someone who was capable of being there for you totally.' He turned back around and looked at her. 'You got a raw deal when you hooked up with me. I was only ever half with you.'

Mikki bit the inside of her mouth before she spoke. 'Where was the other half?'

He gave her a bleak look. 'See that ocean out there?' He pointed to the pounding surf behind him.

She gave a tiny nod. 'Yes…'

'Out there, lost, gone for ever,' he said

Mikki frowned in confusion. 'What do you mean?'

He gave her an embittered grimace. 'Twenty years ago my brother was pulled from that surf. I was on another wave and didn't even know he had been knocked unconscious until it was too late. I got him to hospital but he only lived a week. The life support was turned off while I stood and watched.'

Mikki felt her chest collapse with the weight of the grief she could feel emanating from him. 'Oh, Lewis…'

He dragged a hand across his face, pulling at his features until he looked twenty years older. 'I lost my father the same day.' He gave a grunt of humourless laughter, an ink spill of black humour that was jarring. 'He blamed me for Liam's death. Not that he said anything outright, but I got the message loud and clear. I should have been watching him. I was the older, more experienced surfer.'

Mikki could barely get her voice to work. The sadness she felt in Lewis was palpable. He was showing her a side to himself that she was pretty sure he had shown no one before. 'He was wrong to blame you, Lewis,' she said. 'What happened to your brother was an accident. It had nothing to do with you. What if you hadn't been surfing with him that day? Or what if it had been someone else with him? Would you have blamed them for not seeing what had happened to Liam?'

'I don't know,' he said. 'Maybe, maybe not. All I know is I couldn't stay here any longer. I applied for a scholarship to study medicine in the UK. I had spent a miserable year living with my father and Abby's mother after Liam died. Anna did her best, but it was pretty clear I was in the way. I couldn't take it any more. I couldn't take my father any more.'

'How long is it since you've spoken to your father?'

'Eighteen years.'

Mikki's eyes went wide. 'But that's half of your life!'

He gave her an indifferent look. 'Yeah, it is.'

Mikki studied him for a long moment. 'It's one of the reasons why you're back in Australia, isn't it? This is the closure you're looking for.'

His expression soured. 'If you think I came all this way to fix things with my father, you can forget it. I have better things to do with my time than shoulder the blame for my brother's death. It was an accident. You're right. Hundreds of people lose their lives in the surf every year. It wasn't my fault.'

'But you do blame yourself,' Mikki said gently. 'You've always blamed yourself. That's why you won't allow yourself to feel anything for anyone.'

His hands went to fists at his sides, opening and closing, his knuckles whitening with the pressure. 'Think what you like, Mikki,' he said through tight lips. 'I came back here to prove I could do it. I was no longer willing to hide away on the other side of the world pretending life was cool when it wasn't. I was sick of running away. I want some closure. I admit that. I want to move on. I'm tired of living half a life.'

'Where do I fit into all this?' Mikki asked.

The stiff set of his shoulders slowly loosened as he gave a deep sigh. 'You know something, Mikki? I'm not really sure. I was sure I would come back and everything would fall into place. You would have your life, I would have mine. But it's not like that. We keep intercepting and I don't know how to deal with it.'

She came over to him and placed one of her hands on his arm. 'I wish you had told me about your family,' she said, 'especially about your brother.'

'Why?' he asked, his eyes still ice-cold. 'So you could feel sorry for me? I hate pity parties, Mikki. I'm always the one to leave first.'

Mikki bit down on her lip. 'I think it would have helped me to understand you better. If I had been a little older and a little more mature and not so caught up in my own issues and insecurities, I might have seen it for myself. I'm sorry for that. I'm sorry I didn't stay around long enough to get to know you.'

His hand came down over the top of hers, his fingers warm and strong. 'It wasn't your fault, Mikki,' he said in a softer tone. 'You just met the wrong guy.'

Mikki looked into his eyes and wondered if that was true. He didn't feel wrong to her even now. He felt so right. She couldn't imagine being with anyone else. She didn't want to be with anyone else if she couldn't have him. 'Maybe it was just the wrong time,' she said.

'Maybe...' His hand fell away from her arm. 'You should get some sleep.'

Mikki hesitated. 'Lewis?'

He stepped away, distancing himself both physically and emotionally. 'We both have to work tomorrow,' he said. 'I have a big list with some difficult cases.'

'Don't shut me out,' she said. 'Please don't shut me out when you've only now let me in.'

He came back to her and took her by the upper arms, a hard grip that she was sure would leave bruises. 'Why are you so determined to get your fingers burnt all over again?' he asked. 'I'm not good for you, Mikki. I've messed up your life once. I don't want to do it again.'

'You didn't mess up my life,' she said, blinking back tears. 'I did that all by myself. I love you, Lewis. I don't think I've ever stopped loving you. Making love with you tonight proved it.'

The silence was one of those deafening, endless, painful ones.

Mikki felt her heart tighten as the mask slipped back over Lewis's face. He let her arms go and stepped back as if she had slapped him.

'You're confusing sex with love, Mikki,' he said. 'Women do it all the time. Practically every woman I have ever slept with has told me they loved me. It means nothing. It's just a way for women to justify giving their bodies to someone.'

A trio of anger and jealousy and hurt came to Mikki's rescue. 'Just how many women have there been?' she asked.

'You have no right to ask that,' he said, with an arctic blast of his eyes. 'You lost that right the day you walked out on our relationship.'

'You could have begged me to come back to you.'

'Beg?' His brow lifted in a disdainful arc. 'Here's the thing, Mikki. I don't beg. That's at least one thing you should have known about me, and seven years on, it hasn't changed.'

Mikki watched as he strode out of the room, leaving her alone with her regrets and self-recriminations, like ghosts all pointing their accusing fingers at her.

CHAPTER NINE

IT WAS three in the morning when Mikki heard him moving about the house. He was trying to be quiet about it but she had a sixth sense where he was concerned. She recalled with a pang of sadness and regret all the times in the past when she had found him up at all hours, reading or blanking, watching television without the sound, or on one or two occasions just staring into space. He had always said it was because of the difficult cases he had been working on and she had believed him. Why wouldn't she? Neurosurgery was one of the most demanding of specialties. Was that why he had chosen it, because of his brother's death through a head injury? Was this his way of redeeming himself, by saving thousands of lives that otherwise would not have been saved? No wonder he was so single-mindedly driven, so focussed and intent on being the best in his field. He was fearless in the face of intricate surgery, and yet that fearlessness masked a man who was dealing with a tragic past in the only way he knew how: by shutting it out.

Mikki slipped on a robe and padded out to the lounge. He was standing staring at the moonlit ocean but he turned when she came in.

'Sorry, did I wake you?' he asked.

'Not really,' she said. 'I'm a light sleeper.'

He ran a hand through his hair and from the state of it she could tell it wasn't the first time that night he had done so. 'You should go back to bed,' he said. 'You look tired.'

'You look pretty worn out yourself.'

He gave her a movement of his lips, not a smile, not a grimace but something in between. 'No one looks their best at three in the morning,' he said.

Mikki came further into the room. 'Do you want a cup of hot milk or hot chocolate or something?' she asked.

Something passed through his eyes, a memory, a flashback, bringing a small smile to his mouth. 'My mother used to make Liam and me hot chocolate when we couldn't sleep,' he said. 'Even after all this time, whenever I taste chocolate I think of her.'

Mikki felt her heart squeeze. 'You told me when we met you couldn't remember her,' she said. 'You said you were too young when she died.'

His eyes flickered again. 'I was four,' he said. 'Liam was only two. I remember more than I want to. It would have been easier to have been like Liam, who couldn't even recall what she looked like. I remembered everything. The way she smiled, the way she hugged me so tightly, as if she knew our time together was limited... the way she smelled like spring flowers...'

'You told me when we met she died in an accident,' Mikki said after a small pause.

He met her gaze, the cold, hard look in them driving a blade of ice through her chest. 'No, it was no accident,' he said. 'My father insisted she have an abortion. Back in those days it wasn't so easy to have one, or at least not by someone who knew what they were doing. She got septicaemia and died.'

Mikki stared at him in horror. 'But…but why did your father insist on her having one?'

His mouth was a tight bloodless line. 'Because he didn't believe the child was his.'

She swallowed painfully. 'But it was his, wasn't it?'

'I don't know and I don't really care,' he said. 'He should never have forced her to get rid of her child.'

Mikki was starting to see why he had offered to marry her without question. Why he hadn't once suggested a way out of their dilemma. 'When I lost our baby…'

'I wasn't able to help you with that, Mikki,' he said. 'It threw me. I just couldn't handle it. I'm sorry you had to deal with that alone. It took me years to work out why I reacted like that. I blocked out what I was feeling. I had to. I've done it since I was a kid. It's the only way I knew how to cope with things. Liam's death made it a million times worse. I couldn't vocalise my grief. I just pretended it hadn't happened. I became someone else, someone who was alone and wanted it that way. It was much better than thinking about the family I'd once had and subsequently lost.'

Mikki moved over to him, wrapping her arms around his waist. He was ramrod stiff, hard and unyielding, but after a moment or two he put his arms around her and drew her close, his head coming down on the top of her head.

'I envied you, Mikki,' he said after a long silence. 'I realise no family is perfect, but you had both of your parents while you were growing up. I know their marriage wasn't totally happy but you had each of them backing you at every turn. They wanted the best for you. They still want the best for you.'

'I must have seemed so spoilt and self-indulgent back then,' Mikki said.

She felt him smile against her hair. 'No, just young,' he said. 'You were so young and innocent, too young and innocent for someone as bitter and twisted as me.'

She looked up at him. 'I'm glad you told me about your mother,' she said. 'She must have loved you and your brother very much.'

'She did,' Lewis said. 'But in some ways I think she was lucky to have died rather than go through the loss of Liam. At least she was spared that.'

Mikki gently stroked his unshaven jaw. 'You've carried all this alone for so long,' she said, struggling to hold back tears. 'No one should have to face all that without support. Your father should have been there for you, no matter what. That's what parents are supposed to do.'

He blotted one of her tears with the pad of his thumb. 'I can never remember being all that close to my father,' he said. 'Liam was his favourite. I had no real problem with it. I had been closer to my mother. I think it's like that in lots of families. It's about the meshing of personalities, just like in any other relationship. Some people get on better than others. It's just a fact of life.

'I was twelve when I found out the circumstances of my mother's death. I overheard my father arguing with his sister. Our already difficult relationship became even trickier after that. And then when Liam died…well, that was the final straw.'

Mikki drew close again, pressing her cheek against the solid wall of his chest. 'I think it's amazing what you've done with your life,' she said. 'You've helped so many people, saved so many lives, even though you've had it tougher than anyone should ever have it.'

'Yeah, well, it was no picnic at times,' he said dryly. 'But I survived.'

She looked up at him again, one of her hands reaching up to trace the ridge of his scar just above his eyebrow. 'How did you get this?'

His expression contorted with the pain of remembering. 'An argument with my father. We both said things that no father or son should ever say to each other. He lost his temper. He'd been drinking and I got under his skin. He threw a punch that I couldn't block in time. I walked out the following day and never went back.'

She stroked the side of his face again. 'I'm so sorry I didn't understand what you'd been through. No wonder you wanted to forget about it and move on with your life.'

He placed his hand over hers and held it to his face. 'Lots of people have hard lives. Up until Liam died my life was going along reasonably well. His death threw everything out of kilter. My way of coping was to walk away. My father's way was to apportion blame and then get down to re-creating another family. It sickened me that he thought he could replace Liam.'

'But Abby is such a lovely girl and you surely don't regret she's your half-sister?'

'No, of course not,' he said. 'I just worry about her stuck with my father now her mother's moved to Perth to be with her new partner. Abby lives in a flat with friends but I know she still feels responsible for making sure our father isn't alone too much. She's entitled to her own life. She shouldn't have to give up hers for him.'

'Is that one of the reasons you came back to Australia?' Mikki asked. 'To keep a protective eye on her?'

He gently cupped her face, holding her eyes with the blue intensity of his. 'That amongst other things,' he said.

She moistened her lips, her heart beginning to pick up its pace when she saw the way his eyes darkened. 'Do you still want that hot chocolate?' she asked.

Lewis's gaze dropped to her mouth and his arms slowly but surely tightened around her. 'Not right now,' he said, and covered her lips with his.

It was a deep kiss, not just physically but emotionally. Mikki could feel the unleashing of much more than desire as his tongue played with hers. Her body leapt to fervent life, like tinder to a flame, her skin erupting with heat as his mouth fed hungrily off hers. The urgency of his kiss ramped up her need of him, making her skin tingle with want as his hands moved to cup her face. She felt the bristle of his unshaven skin scrape her softer one but she didn't care. She pressed herself closer, kissing him back with the same heated urgency, using her tongue and even her teeth in little nippy bites to show him how much she wanted him.

His hands moved from her face to skim over her body, stopping briefly at her breasts, cupping them and then shaping them possessively. Her nipples jumped to attention, her breathing becoming ragged as he deepened the kiss even further. He made a sound in the back of his throat, a primal sound of a male close to mating. Mikki gave a whimper of response, her inner core contracting with a pulse of longing that was so intense she felt she would die if he didn't finish this the way she wanted him to.

'This is madness,' Lewis said, working his way back up to her mouth with hot, moist kisses. 'We really should stop before this gets out of hand.'

Mikki nibbled on his neck and then his earlobe. 'I know but I'm enjoying it too much.'

'Me too,' he said, bringing his mouth back to hers.

She gave herself up to his drugging kiss, her body melting against his as he drew her down to the carpeted floor. He came down on top of her, his weight pinning her beneath him, making her intimately aware of his need.

He parted her robe, and then slipped the shoestring straps of her nightdress down over her shoulder, exposing her breast. His eyes darkened before he lowered his mouth to her, sucking on her, drawing on her until she was clinging to him shamelessly. She ran her hands over his naked back and shoulders, delighting in the play of hard muscles under her fingertips.

He moved to her other breast, making her squirm with delight as he swirled his tongue over her before drawing her nipple into his mouth.

She went in search of him, pushing away his boxer shorts to claim him. He made another sound in his throat as her fingers closed over him, a sound of pleasure and anticipation.

'I don't have a condom,' he reminded her somewhat hoarsely.

'No matter,' she said, wriggling out from under him and giving him a sultry look.

His eyes glinted when she pushed him down, using the flat of her hand against his chest. 'You sure about this, Mikki?' he asked.

'Perfectly sure. I'm on the Pill.'

Lewis was beyond thought of anything but of how wonderful it felt to be subjected to such an earth-shattering assault on his senses by Mikki's soft lips and little kitten tongue.

His breathing was all over the place when she came back up to drape herself over him, her tawny-brown eyes alight with feminine pride. 'Good?' she asked, trailing a lazy finger down over his nose.

'Better than good.' He captured her finger and drew it into his mouth, sucking on it just as she had done to him. She wriggled on top of him, stirring his body all over again. He knew he should have pulled away. He knew he should have moved so the temptation to slip inside that delectable honeyed warmth was out of his reach, but he didn't. Instead, he rolled her under him in a swift movement that made her gasp, his body surging into hers like a missile finding its target.

She wrapped around him like a tight fist, the rippled walls of her body holding him as if she never wanted to let him go.

He thrust deeper, caught on a tide of longing that was unstoppable. Every movement set off explosions of feeling inside him, the friction of their bodies so intense he had trouble holding back. He caressed her with his fingers, the wet swollen heart of her responding to him instantly. He felt every convulsion of her release, the clutching of her body triggering his own. He emptied himself, his body pumping every last drop of his essence until he was lying spent over her, his breathing uneven, his heart thumping, his skin peppered with goose-bumps of delight.

They moved through to the bedroom and he lay with her wrapped in his arms for a long time after she had fallen asleep. Her honey-brown hair tickled his chest where she had laid her head, but he didn't move away. He breathed in the scent of her shampoo, a fragrant of mix of jasmine and some other spring flower he couldn't quite recognise. She nestled against him with a soft murmur, just as she used to do in the past. His heart gave a tiny contraction, an ache for how much he had missed her over the years. He'd always been able to ignore it in the past, but now it was different. He wasn't on the other side of the world any more. He was here, working with her, sleeping with her…loving her? He frowned at the thought. She had said she loved him the last time and look how long that had lasted. Love was something he tried to keep away from. It complicated things. He loved his job, and he certainly loved Abby who was so young and bright and cheerful, just like Liam had been before that fateful day. Lewis had loved his mother. He had loved her and yet lost her, just like his brother. Was he one of those unfortunate people destined to lose everyone he loved? He had always felt it was better to keep his feelings locked away, to ignore them, to deny them any foothold.

He thought of Mark Upton and his love for his wife Jenny. It was painful to watch. It was devastating to think that could be him one day, vulnerable, living in dread, hoping for a miracle, not sure if one was going to be delivered or not. Mikki had accused him of being too positive with his patients, but he couldn't bear to knock away people's hope. There was always hope. He had spent the last decade of his life learning how to operate to a standard so high so that hope became a reality for at least some of the patients who had been given none.

Mikki moved in her sleep, snaking her slim arms around him as she snuggled in even closer. Her lips moved against the naked skin of his chest in another soft murmur of sound. He stroked her silky hair, pressing a soft kiss to the top of her head.

'That's nice...' she said, and looked up at him sleepily.

He stilled the movement of his fingers in her hair. 'I thought you were asleep.'

Her lips curved upwards. 'I was...sort of,' she said. 'I was drifting in and out. I thought I was dreaming but then I realised you were here with me, holding me.'

Lewis brushed her hair back from her face, his heart giving another tight contraction. 'I like watching you sleep,' he said.

'Why?'

He shrugged but kept playing with her hair. 'Not sure.'

'Have you watched your other lovers sleeping?' she asked.

Lewis let out a breath. 'I haven't spent the whole night with anyone since you left.'

Her eyes flared in surprise. 'Why's that?'

'It didn't feel right, I guess,' he said.

A shadow passed over her face and she looked down at his chest rather than meet his eyes. 'How many women have there been since me?' she asked.

'Mikki, I don't think that's something I should—'

Her tawny brown eyes flashed at him as she brought her head up. 'Did you love any of them?'

He felt his jaw tighten. 'No of course not.'

'Did you tell them about me?'

'No.'

'Why not?'

'Mikki, this is a pointless conversation,' Lewis said, moving away. 'I had lovers from time to time. Opportunities arose and I took them. I'm human after all. If you can't deal with it then don't ask. Leave the past where it belongs.'

The silence throbbed for a few seconds.

Lewis turned and saw a track of tears making their way down Mikki's cheeks. He swore and rolled back to gather her close. 'Don't cry, Mikki,' he said. 'I can't bear to see you cry.'

She brushed at her eyes with her hands. 'I'm not crying.'

He leaned forward to gently kiss her forehead. 'You have no need to be jealous, sweetheart.'

She sent him a pouting look. 'I'm not jealous.'

He held her chin steady, locking his gaze with hers. 'I would be worried if you weren't,' he said.

A little frown tugged at her brow. 'Why?'

He traced a fingertip down her nose. 'I would be insanely jealous if things were the other way around.'

'I wasn't consciously saving myself for you,' she said with the same little pout.

He gave her a ghost of a smile as he brushed his knuckles down her cheek. 'Maybe not, but it's nice to know I'm still your first and only lover.'

Her eyes misted over again. 'No one ever seemed to come up to your standard,' she said. 'You spoilt me for anyone else. I tried to date, I really did, but no one ever came close to you.'

Lewis cupped her face in his hands. 'I've made my own fair share of comparisons, Mikki.'

'You have?'

'Sure I have.'

'And?'

He kissed her on the mouth. 'You're back in my life, aren't you?'

That little shadow passed over her face again. 'For now.'

'That's all I can offer right now, Mikki,' he said. 'It's too early to say where this will go.'

'Because you don't believe in love.'

'I've never said that.'

'You're incapable of it, then.'

'I haven't said that either,' Lewis said.

She turned away from him, her body curled up like a comma.

He stroked a hand down her naked back, smiling to

himself when she gave a little shiver before she turned back over. He pulled her into his arms, taking her mouth with his, filling her with the thickness of his arousal, taking her to paradise with him until finally, totally spent, they fell asleep.

When Mikki woke the sun was streaming in through her bedroom window. She turned her head to watch Lewis still sleeping. His eyes still bore the shadows of a man who worked too long and too hard. She reached out with a soft fingertip and stroked the stubble on his jaw, her belly giving a little flutter as his raspy skin caught on her softer one, reminding her of how different their bodies were and yet how sensually compatible. She could still feel where he had filled her. The sensual silk of his life force a reminder of how deeply intimate they had been. No barriers this time. Was it symbolic of how they had moved forward from the secrets and omissions of the past?

He opened his eyes and turned his head to look at her. 'How come you look even more beautiful in the morning with your hair all mussed up and a linen crease on your cheek?' he asked.

Mikki put a hand to her face. 'Have I? Where?'

He traced a slow finger down the side of her left cheek. 'Right there,' he said.

She chewed at her lip, trying to ignore the way her skin was tingling from his touch. 'I'm going to be late if I don't get out of bed in the next few minutes.'

His hand moved down to capture her chin, his eyes meshing with hers, not cold and distant but warm, smouldering. 'If someone needs you urgently, they will call you,' he said, rolling her onto her back and coming over her. 'Anyway, right now I'm the one who needs you urgently.'

Mikki gave a little gasp as he possessed her in one strong thrust. He moved within her, building the pace, carrying her along with him in a breakneck race to the finish. She clung to him, her body racked with shudders of want that made her totally breathless. It was passionate and raw, racy and reckless, again with no barrier between them. She felt herself come apart seconds before he did, her high cries of release a perfect counterpoint to his bass groan of pleasure as he spilled himself.

Mikki didn't want to move. She could have stayed in bed in his arms all day but the ringtone of Lewis's mobile shattered the sensual spell, reminding them both they had jobs to go to, patients to see and support.

'Damn,' he said, reaching past her to pick up his phone from the bedside table where he had left it the night before. 'Looks like I am the one someone needs urgently.' He looked at the screen and frowned as he answered it. 'Abby? Hey, what's wrong?'

Mikki was close enough to hear his half-sister's wobbling voice.

'Lewis, it's Dad,' Abby said. 'He collapsed at home. I'm at the hospital with him now. He's being assessed in the emergency department. Can you come? I can't face this on my own. He's sick, Lewis. He's been sick for ages and he hasn't told anyone. I don't know what to do.'

'I'll be there as soon as I can,' Lewis said. 'Just try and stay calm.'

Later Mikki couldn't quite recall how they both got

showered and dressed and arrived at the hospital within the next twenty minutes. It all seemed a bit of a blur. Lewis was mostly silent, obviously preparing himself for facing his father for the first time in eighteen years. She tried to talk to him, to offer her support at the very least, but he was stony-faced and cut her off with monosyllabic responses.

'Would you like me to come with you?' she ventured again as he parked her car in the hospital car park. 'I'd like to be there for you and for Abby.'

Lewis's gaze met hers grimly. 'Haven't you got better things to do?'

She reached for his hand and gripped it firmly. 'I'd like to be there for you, Lewis, if you'll let me.'

He pulled his hand away. 'Suit yourself.'

Mikki followed him into the hospital, determined to do what she could, if for no other reason than to better understand the enigmatic nature of the man she loved.

Robert Beck was being assessed by Jake Chandler, the new director of A and E. Jake had ordered a CAT scan, which was being conducted as they arrived.

Abby jumped up from the chair she was sitting on in the empty cubicle and threw herself into Lewis's arms. 'I'm sorry for being such a drama queen but I had no idea he was even ill,' she said. 'I knew he'd been losing weight but I thought it was because he's been drinking rather than eating. I think I told you he drinks too much. It's probably nothing, maybe a bit of indigestion or something.'

Mikki watched as Lewis stroked his sister's dark head where it lay against his broad chest. 'Whatever it is, Dr Chandler will sort it out one way or the other,' he said.

Jake Chandler twitched aside the cubicle curtain as he came in. Like Lewis, he was tall and had the regular dark good looks that made many a female heart flutter, both patients and staff. Mikki had done her fair share of double-takes, but for some reason Jake had never appealed to her. He was known to be a bit of a playboy. He seemed to have a different girlfriend every month or so. But while his personal life might not be to her taste, she had nothing negative to say about his professional skills. He was a first-class A and E doctor and many a time he had diagnosed a condition that others had missed, or had saved a life that had been thought unsalvageable.

Jake flashed Mikki his perfect white smile before he extended his hand to Lewis. 'I'm sorry we're meeting under circumstances like this,' he said. 'Your father is having a CAT scan. I've sent off some bloods. He came in jaundiced. It seems he's been like this before. Do you know who his regular GP is?'

'I have no idea,' Lewis said. 'Do you, Abby?'

Abby chewed her lip. 'I don't think Dad's been to a GP since he and Mum got divorced. He's never really taken good care of himself.'

Jake nodded. 'Yes, a lot of older men are like that. Well, we'll see what the scan shows. I'll keep you posted. I think we'll admit him for a few days just to be on the safe side. He seems rather malnourished. He lives alone, is that correct?'

'Yes,' Abby answered. 'I moved out a few months ago to flat-share with friends closer to university. I guess I should have been keeping a closer eye on him.'

'He's a grown man,' Jake said with a reassuring smile. He turned back to Lewis. 'I hear you're doing amazing things on the neuro ward.'

'Just doing my job,' Lewis said.

'Well, it's great to have you on board,' Jake said. 'Ah, here's your father coming back now. I'll leave you to have a chat with him while I have a word with the radiographer.'

Mikki watched as one of the orderlies wheeled in the bed from the X-ray department. Lewis's father had the same long, rangy build as Lewis, but that was as far as the likeness went. His father was severely jaundiced, his skin a sallow, yellowish colour, even to the whites of his eyes. He was thin; his skin stretched over his bones like a sheet draped over a piece of angular furniture.

'Dad?' Abby grasped her father's blue-veined hand as the bed was wheeled into the cubicle. 'I hope you don't mind but Lewis is here.'

CHAPTER TEN

Mikki stood on one side as Lewis came face to face with his father. His expression was shuttered but, then, perhaps not surprisingly, his father's was no different.

'I suppose you've come to gloat,' Robert said sourly. 'To have a look at what a miserable wreck your old man has become.'

'How long have you been unwell?' Lewis asked with cool composure.

His father closed his eyes. 'Long enough to know I'm dying. Don't matter what tests or scans you doctors run. I know my days are numbered.'

'Are you in any pain?' Lewis asked.

Robert opened his eyes and looked at his son. 'That would please you, wouldn't it? To have me suffer for my sins.'

Lewis's jaw tightened so much a tic developed at the side of his mouth. 'That's not what I want at all,' he said.

His father gave a grunt and then closed his eyes again. 'I don't want to keep you from your work. No doubt you've got better things to do than hang around here. I don't need anyone's pity, certainly not yours.'

'You're right,' Lewis said. 'I do have better things to do.'

He moved out of the cubicle without even acknowledging Mikki on his way past.

'Dad?' Abby gave her father's hand another squeeze. 'There's someone I think you ought to meet. Lewis's fiancée…I mean ex-fiancée, Mikki Landon. Remember I told you about her? She and Lewis met in London seven years ago.'

Robert opened his eyes and looked at Mikki standing by the bedside. 'So you're the one he let get away,' he said.

Mikki offered her hand. 'I'm sorry to meet you when you're not well,' she said. 'But you're in good hands. Dr Chandler and Lewis will make sure you get the best help possible.'

'If you had any sense, you'd stay away from my son,' Robert said. 'He'll end up hurting you. It's what he does best.'

'I can take care of myself, Mr Beck,' Mikki said.

He curled his top lip, a feeble attempt at a mocking smile. 'He has an unforgiving streak in him, proud too. Too proud for his own good.'

'He has a right to be proud of his achievements,' Mikki said. 'He's one of the world's most respected neurosurgeons.'

Robert grunted again. 'Tell him not to bother seeing me again. I have nothing to say to him. Not after all this time.'

Mikki pressed her lips together as she saw Abby's eyes glistening with tears. 'Isn't it time to put the past aside?' she asked, turning back to Robert. 'It's been

eighteen years since you saw Lewis. He's your son, Mr
Beck. He's your flesh and blood.'

'No point trying to play happy families with us,'
Robert said. 'Lewis hates me. Let's leave it at that. I
can live with it. I have lived with it for many a long
year.'

'I don't believe that,' Mikki said. 'I don't believe
Lewis hates you any more than you hate him.'

Robert made another attempt at a smile but it was hu
mourless. 'You seem a nice girl, Mikki,' he said. 'Don't
go getting your heart broken, will you? He will walk
away. It's what he does best. He'll just walk away and
never look back.'

'I was the one who walked away,' Mikki said.

'I bet he didn't come after you.'

'No… No, he didn't.'

He turned his head on the pillow to face her, his
expression unutterably sad. 'I should have gone after
him,' he said. 'I thought of it. I even booked a flight a
couple of times.'

'Why didn't you go?' Mikki asked.

He let out a long sigh that rattled inside his chest. 'It's
a Beck trait, Mikki,' he said. 'Pride, stubborn pride.'

Jake Chandler came back in at that point and Mikki
stood up to leave.

'Don't go,' Abby said.

Mikki felt uncomfortable but stayed to support Abby
as Jake delivered the results of the CAT scan. Robert had
advanced pancreatic cancer. He had just months to live.
He took the news stoically, hardly a muscle moving on
his face, reminding Mikki of Lewis so much she felt her
heart constrict as if someone was clamping it in a vice.

Once Jake had left she stayed with Abby and her father for a few minutes before a call came through for her. She promised to visit Robert once he was transferred to the medical ward and, giving Abby a hug, left.

Mrs Yates, the elderly patient in ICU, was failing. Her organs were shutting down, and after talking to the old woman's daughters Mikki felt it was time to speak John Bramley again about the decision to withdraw life support.

'I totally agree with you, Mikki,' John said over the phone. 'But the son is still insisting on pushing ahead. I think nature will take care of things, quite frankly. I've got another case in Theatre before I can get down. Are you OK to speak to the son? He's probably going to want to have a face-to-face. Don't let him upset you. I don't like the fellow. I think he doesn't give a fig about what his mother would have wanted.'

'I'll be fine,' Mikki said, and soon after ended the call.

As if on cue, a man in his early fifties appeared at the door of the office. 'Dr Landon?' he said. 'I'm Garry Yates.'

Mikki offered her hand but he ignored it. She let it drop back by her side and suggested they move through to one of the family counselling rooms outside the unit.

Garry Yates followed her to the counselling room but once there refused to sit down. He pointed a finger at her, twin flags of colour rising in his cheeks. 'I want my mother to be kept alive,' he said. 'Under no circumstances is she to have her life support withdrawn, no matter what my sisters say to the contrary.'

Mikki took a calming breath. 'I understand your pain at this time, Mr Yates, but your mother is eighty-seven years old. She is going downhill rapidly. She isn't going to recover. Her vital signs have worsened daily. Your sisters felt it would be in keeping with your mother's wishes to let her go in peace while they could be there with her, and you too, of course.'

'Who do you think you are?' he asked. 'God?'

'I'm sorry, Mr Yates, I know this is a difficult decision to make at any age. But your mother's condition is unsalvageable. There is no hope of recovery. I think you and your sisters should prepare yourselves for the worst.'

'This won't be the last you'll be hearing from me if you turn off that ventilator,' Garry threatened. He wrenched open the door, throwing at her before he left, 'You'd better watch your back, Dr Landon.'

Mikki flinched as the door snapped shut.

Lewis came into the unit to check on Jenny Upton, and once he was satisfied things were improving, he asked Kylie where Mikki was.

'She came back from a meeting with a relative a few minutes ago looking like thunder,' Kylie said. 'I think she's gone to the doctors' room for a break.'

'Which relative?' Lewis asked, looking up from the notes he was jotting down.

'Mrs Yates's son,' she said. 'I might be speaking out of turn but I don't like the man one little bit. It seems to me he doesn't love his mother so much as her money.

Apparently he's been cut out of the will and he wants her to wake up long enough to rewrite it. I heard him shouting at Mikki when I walked past the counselling room. He was threatening her. I wanted to call Security but Mikki said to leave it.'

Lewis handed Kylie the patient's file. 'I'll go and have a word with her. Call me if there's any change with Jenny Upton.'

'Will do.'

Mikki was waiting for a fresh brew of coffee to filter through the machine when Lewis came in to the doctors' room.

'I heard Mrs Yates's son has been threatening you,' he said. 'Are you all right?'

She gave him a brief, tight smile. 'Now that I've simmered down a bit.'

'You should report him,' Lewis said, frowning heavily.

'He's just feeling the strain of letting go,' she said. She picked up the coffee pot. 'Would you like a coffee?'

He scraped a hand through his hair. 'Yeah, that sounds like a good idea.'

Mikki poured them both a cup and brought it to where he was sitting. 'Have you been back to see your father?' she asked.

He stared into the contents of his cup. 'No.'

'Have you spoken to Jake Chandler about the results of the scan?'

'Yeah.' He stirred the coffee into a whirlpool that sent some liquid over the rim and into the saucer.

She sat down beside him, placing a gentle hand on the top of his thigh. 'I think you should go and see him.'

His blue eyes met hers. 'Don't get involved in the train wreck of my family, Mikki.'

'You're very like him, you know,' she said.

He gave a rough grunt. 'Kill me now.'

'You're proud and hate admitting when you get it wrong,' she said. 'You don't do emotion well. You shut down when things get to you. You push people away when you really should be drawing them closer.'

Lewis got up from the chair and paced the floor. 'You can keep your pop psychology for the psych ward. It's completely wasted on me.'

Mikki got to her feet and blocked his pacing by putting her hand on his arm. 'You have to see him, Lewis. You have to make peace with him. Let him at least die in peace.'

His brooding frown brought his dark brows together over his eyes. 'Stay out of it, Mikki,' he said, pulling away from her. 'Just stay out of it.'

'No, I won't stay out of it,' she said. 'I think he wants to sort things out with you. Why else would he have come to this hospital?'

'He's got health insurance. This hospital has a private wing. Big deal.'

Mikki gave him a look. 'This is not the only co-located hospital in Sydney. I think he came here because he knew you were here.'

'Abby probably organised it when she found him collapsed at home.'

'Maybe she did, but he could have refused, couldn't

he?' she said. 'If he didn't want anything to do with you, do you really think he would agree to be taken to the very hospital where you were on staff?'

He sent his hand through his hair again. 'He pushes all my buttons,' he said bitterly. 'Every word that comes out of his mouth has a sting in its tail.'

'He does that because he's hurting,' Mikki said. 'If you read the subtext, I think he's saying something completely different.'

'What did he say to you to get you on his side so quickly?' he asked with a surly look.

Mikki let out a breath. 'Lewis, he was going to visit you in London. He said he'd even gone so far as booking tickets.'

His expression stilled. 'He told you that?'

She nodded. 'I felt sad for him. I think he has a lot of regrets. A lot of people do when they know they are coming to the end of their life. Who of us wouldn't want to change things if we could?'

Lewis moved to the windows to look at the car park below. 'I'm not ready for this,' he said. He swore again, viciously, his hands in tight fists by his sides. 'I don't want to deal with this right now.'

Mikki came up behind him and stroked him between his stiff shoulder blades. 'You have to deal with it. You can't walk away from it. He needs you, Lewis. He really does. I'm sure of it. Abby does too. She shouldn't have to cope with this on her own.'

Lewis turned around to face her. 'I came back for Abby, not my father.'

She looked up into his eyes. 'You came back for lots

of reasons, Lewis. You're just not ready to admit to all of them.'

His lips moved in a semblance of a wry smile. 'You think you've got me all worked out, don't you, Mikki?'

'I'm working on it,' she said. 'You're like a book I couldn't understand the first time I read it. It's only now on a second reading I'm starting to understand what makes you the man you are.'

He put his hands on her shoulders, his fingers digging in almost painfully. 'I wish it had been me that had died that day,' he said. 'I think Liam would have coped with our father much better than I did. He would have stuck it out. He would have found a way to get through it. I just couldn't do it. I had to get away. I couldn't face the grief, not just my own but my father's. It was too much. He wanted a scapegoat. I was it. I took it for so long and then I just had to leave. I wanted to put it all behind me, to forget it ever happened. But you can never really escape, can you? It becomes part of you. There's not a day I don't think of my brother. What he might be doing if he'd had the chance to reach his potential. He might have been married now with kids. That's the part that gets me most. He was the one who was the people person. I was the more reserved, quiet one. He loved life. He was the life and soul of any party. He wanted it all and in the end he got nothing. He's lying in a grave while I drag myself through life wishing…wishing it could be different.'

Mikki put her arms around his waist. 'But you've made your life count. You've done so much to help other people. You haven't wasted a moment. You've worked hard and achieved things, not just for yourself but for Liam too.'

He pulled her against him, holding her tightly. 'I should have come after you when you left,' he said. 'I should have done everything in my power to bring you back.'

'It wasn't our time, Lewis,' she said. 'We were on different paths.'

His sigh was like a breeze through her hair. 'Did you call off our engagement because your parents were against our marriage?' he asked.

Mikki pushed back to look up at him. 'Is that what you thought?'

'It crossed my mind.'

She frowned at him. 'I ended it because I didn't know for sure you were in love with me. The baby was the only thing holding us together. If we had married, baby or no baby, we would probably have been divorced by now.'

'You think so?'

'I know so,' she said. 'Bringing a child into an already tenuous relationship is a recipe for disaster. My parents married because of me. I only found that out a couple of years ago. My mother fell pregnant and my father felt compelled to do the right thing by her. They wasted so many years of their lives trying to make it work.'

He looked down at her with a frown on his face. 'I felt devastated when you lost the baby,' he said. 'I know I didn't communicate it but I felt as if it was my fault, that I had jinxed yet another life. I retreated into myself, pretending it had never happened. It wasn't the most mature way to deal with something as big and life-changing as that. But it was the only way I knew how to deal with it. I shut down. I closed off.'

'I thought you were relieved when I told you I had lost the baby,' Mikki said.

'As awful as this sounds, I think in a way I was a bit relieved,' he said. 'I felt so guilty about getting you pregnant. You had fallen behind in your studies and I knew it was my fault. Losing the baby freed you to get back to your career. I didn't want to stand in the way of that. I know I should have talked things through with you but I was so used to distancing myself it was impossible to get the words out.'

'We both made mistakes,' Mikki said. 'But it doesn't matter now. What matters now is sorting out things with your father. It's important, Lewis, surely you see that?'

He drew in a long breath and slid his hands down to encircle her wrists. 'I'll go and see him when I finish my shift,' he said heavily.

Mikki smiled and reaching up planted a soft kiss on his mouth. 'I think I'll head down now and take Abby out for a coffee. She'll need a break by now. She's been down there with him since early this morning.'

Lewis brought her hands up to his mouth and pressed a kiss to her bent knuckles. 'Don't go home without me, OK? My car is being delivered today but I don't want you to drive home without me. I've got used to having you around.'

'I'm not going anywhere too far away this time,' she said, and pressed another soft kiss to his mouth.

* * *

Mikki met Abby in the hospital café and suggested they go outside to get some fresh air once they'd had a drink. 'You look exhausted, Abby,' she said. 'You don't have to stay by your father's bed side all day.'

'He's got no one else,' Abby said. 'He's got no friends to speak of. There's just me and…well, Lewis, I guess.' She stopped walking and looked at Mikki. 'Do you think he will visit Dad?'

'He told me he was going to go down after he finishes today,' Mikki said. 'I kind of talked him into it.'

Abby raised her brows. 'Wow, you really must have some sway with him after all.'

Mikki felt her cheeks colour up and began walking again. 'Lewis is his own man, as I'm sure you already know,' she said.

'Tell me about it,' Abby said, falling into step beside her. 'They are so alike it's uncanny. I would hate Lewis to end up like my father, though, alone and lonely and too proud to ask anyone for help.'

'They've both had a lot of bad stuff happen to them,' Mikki said. 'People deal with things in their own way. That's when communication can break down so quickly and so tragically.'

'Are you getting back together with Lewis?' Abby asked. 'I know he spent the night at your place last night.'

Mikki faltered over her response. 'I…I… It's… I'm not sure…'

'Not sure about what?'

'Not sure what Lewis wants,' Mikki said.

'He cares for you, Mikki, I know he does.'

Mikki turned to look at her. 'Has he said that to you?'

Abby smiled knowingly. 'He doesn't need to. Anyway, you know Lewis. He plays his cards pretty close to his chest. It's just he's never looked at anyone the way he looks at you. I think he's in love with you. I think he's always been in love with you but he doesn't know how to express it.'

'All it takes is three little words,' Mikki said dryly.

'I know, but you have to remember that Lewis has lost just about everyone he has loved,' Abby said. 'That's why he's so protective over me. I totally get it, though. He blames himself for Liam's death. Who wouldn't? It's perfectly understandable but in time he has to learn to let it go.'

'Has your father ever openly blamed Lewis for Liam's death?' Mikki asked.

'I think in the early days he did,' Abby said. 'Mum got pretty fed up with it. It's one of the reasons she left in the end. I think my father is the one who felt guilty. From what I've gathered, he was a pretty absent father for the boys. They were mostly brought up by nannies after their mother died. He left them to their own devices a lot of the time. But here's the kicker: he was away the weekend Liam got hurt, surfing.'

Mikki stopped again to look at Abby. 'Where was he?'

'At some health spa detox-type retreat,' Abby said. 'My mother insisted he go to sort himself out. He got the first flight back he could but Liam never regained consciousness.'

'So he projected his guilt on Lewis,' Mikki said.

'Pretty much,' Abby said. 'I think that's why my parents' marriage was doomed to fail. They both felt guilty about how things turned out that weekend. The sad thing is Mum was only trying to help my father tone down his drinking. In the end it only made things much worse.'

'Poor Lewis,' Mikki said. 'And poor you, caught up in all of it.'

Abby gave her a resigned smile. 'I sorted out my stuff a long time ago. I know my father isn't perfect but he's tried to be a good dad. We've had our moments, but now I just want to see him at peace.'

'It's not good news about his health,' Mikki said. 'How are you dealing with that?'

'It will be easier to deal with now that Lewis is home,' Abby said. 'I don't know how I would have coped without his support. He's the best big brother a girl could have.'

'He's certainly pretty special,' Mikki said, smiling softly.

Abby tilted her head as she looked at her again. 'You love him, don't you?' she asked.

Mikki coloured up again. 'I told myself I wouldn't be so foolish as to fall for him again, but it's different this time. It's not the same as seven years ago. I've realised lately I hardly knew him then. I was swept up in a romantic fantasy, the excitement of my first love made all the more romantic by it happening abroad. This time I've fallen in love with who Lewis really is: the strong, honourable man who feels deeply but hates showing it.'

'I hope it works out for you both this time around,' Abby said, linking her arm through Mikki's. 'I quite fancy having you as a sister-in-law.'

Mikki smiled but it was shadowed by uncertainty.

'That will depend entirely on Lewis,' she said. 'I'm not sure he's ever wanted to settle down.' *And that is what I want most of all.*

CHAPTER ELEVEN

'MIKKI?' Lewis came into the office where she was writing the fluids up for a patient. 'Do you have a few minutes?'

She closed the folder. 'Of course,' she said. 'My shift is over now in any case. I was just going to fill in time till you were free to leave.'

He stood looking down at her for a long moment without speaking.

Mikki lifted one brow as a prompt. 'Er…is there something you want to say?'

He cleared his throat. 'I'm heading down to see my father,' he said. 'I thought you might like to come with me.'

She looked at him in surprise. 'You want me to be there?'

He shrugged as if he couldn't care either way. 'It's not a big deal. I just thought since we'll be leaving together, it might save time.'

Mikki got to her feet. 'Just let me get my bag from the locker room.'

When she got back Lewis was waiting with his hands thrust in his trouser pockets, standing looking out of the office window to the car park below.

'I'm ready,' she said.

He turned and met her gaze. 'You don't have to do this if you don't want to, Mikki. It's probably wrong of me to drag you into this.'

She came over, pulled one of his hands free and brought it up to her face. 'I want to be there for you, Lewis.'

The edges of his mouth lifted in an almost smile. 'I want you to be there too,' he said.

Robert was complaining volubly to one of the nurses about the hospital food as well as the lack of choice on television.

'If there's anything you particularly want, Mr Beck has authorised for it to be brought to you,' the nurse said as she straightened the covers on the bed. 'You must be very proud of your son. Everyone speaks very highly of him.'

'He's too busy to be of any use to me,' Robert said with a scowl.

'Mr Beck may be one of the busiest specialists in this hospital but he still made time to make sure you had a private room,' the nurse said. 'He had to pull a few strings as there wasn't one available.'

Robert grunted. 'I don't want to be fussed over. I want to be left to die in peace.'

'Ah, here's your son now,' the nurse said.

Lewis thanked her as he came in with Mikki by his side. 'How are you feeling?' he asked his father.

'Felt better,' Robert grumbled, without making eye contact.

'I brought Mikki with me,' Lewis said.

Robert's top lip curled. 'What? Were you too gutless to face me on your own?'

Mikki bit her lip, her eyes going to Lewis. He stood like a marble statue, no expression on his face, apart from that little nerve beating in his lower jaw.

'I thought you might like to get to know her,' he said after a pause.

'What would be the point?' Robert said. 'I won't be around long enough to get to know anybody.'

'You have a terminal illness, but even the terminally ill are still alive,' Lewis said.

Mikki felt her heart surge with love for him. She had never heard it put so poignantly before. It showed her yet again the depths she had overlooked when she had met him seven years ago.

'I don't want to be hooked up to any machines,' Robert said.

'I can organise a "Do not resuscitate" order for you to sign,' Lewis said. 'The doctors looking after you will do their best to make you as comfortable as possible.'

'I'm tired,' Robert said, closing his eyes. 'I'd like to be left alone.'

'I'll come and see you in the morning,' Lewis said.

'I'm sure you've got more important things to do.'

Mikki reached for Lewis's hand and gave it a gentle squeeze. 'Mr Beck?' she said. 'Would you mind very much if I dropped in now and again? I don't want to intrude, but I spent some time with Abby this afternoon and I think she will need Lewis's and my support over the coming weeks or months.'

Robert turned his head to look at her. 'She's all I've

got left,' he said. 'She's a good kid. I wish I'd been a better father, and a better husband to her mother.'

'I'm sure you did your best,' Mikki said. 'No one can ask more of you than that.'

Robert closed his eyes again. 'Sometimes your best isn't good enough, certainly for some people it isn't.'

Mikki touched him briefly on the hand. 'I hope you have a comfortable night,' she said. 'I'll come and see you tomorrow.'

'See you tomorrow,' Lewis said.

His father didn't reply.

Lewis dropped Mikki's hand once they had left his father's room. She felt him retreat into himself. The stony face, the rigid set to his shoulders and the tight line of his mouth warned her to give him some time and space. It was so different from how she would have responded seven years ago. Back then she would have insisted he talk about it, she would have needled him until he lost his temper or said something cutting that would leave her hurt and miserable for days. No wonder things had gone so horribly wrong. She had just been too young and immature to deal with someone as complicated as Lewis.

When they arrived in tandem back at her town house she was torn with wanting him to stay and allowing him space. 'You don't have to stay if you want to be alone, Lewis,' she said as she locked her car.

'You know something?' he said, clicking his own remote device, 'I don't want to be alone. Anyway, I could do with a drink.'

Once inside the house, she organised some wine for

them both and took it out to the balcony, where he was standing looking at the churning surf. 'Here you go,' she said.

Lewis took the glass and downed it in a couple of mouthfuls before handing her back the glass. 'Thanks.'

Mikki chewed at her lips. 'Do you want another?' she asked after a moment.

He gave a rough-sounding laugh. 'And turn out to be a pathetic drunk like my father?'

'He's not a pathetic drunk, Lewis,' she said softly.

He rounded on her, his blue eyes as brittle as ice. 'So you know him so well now, do you? His brand of working-class charm appeals to you, does it?'

She ran her tongue over her dry lips. 'Lewis, I don't want to argue with you.'

'Then keep your opinions to yourself,' he bit out.

She turned to go back inside but before she'd taken half a step he had snagged one of her arms. 'No, don't go,' he said, his voice sounding gruff. 'I'm sorry. I'm taking out my frustration on you. Forgive me.'

Mikki put her hand over his. 'This is a very difficult time for you. I can see that. Your father's dying and he's shutting you out.'

He looked down at her hand on his. 'I should just walk away once and for all.'

'But you won't do that, will you?' she said.

His eyes met hers, holding them for a long moment before he released a heavy sigh. 'No, probably not.'

She moved in to hug him, holding him as close to her as she could. 'You're a really special person, Lewis,' she said. 'I wish I had realised that in the past.'

She felt his chin come to rest on the top of her head, and his arms wrapped around her, holding her as if he never wanted to let her go.

It was a long time before he spoke. 'I must have really hurt you back then...you know...how I handled things.'

Mikki looked up at him. 'I got over it.'

He pushed back to frown at her. 'Did you?'

'Well, maybe not as quickly as I would have liked,' she admitted.

He released her from his hold and stepped back from her, his expression grave. 'Mikki, there's something you should know.'

She frowned. 'About what?'

'Remember the night I ran into you at the restaurant in Bondi?' he said.

'Yes...'

He took a deep breath. 'Mikki, that wasn't a coincidence.'

Her brow furrowed some more. 'It...it wasn't?'

He shook his head. 'I knew you were going to be there at that time with your mother that night.'

Mikki stared at him. 'My mother *told* you we'd be there? Is that why she was so late? Did she set it up? What was she thinking?'

'It wasn't your mother.'

She stared at him some more, trying to get her mind to shuffle through the possibilities. 'Then who was it?'

'Your father.'

Her eyes became round. *'My father?'*

Lewis gave her a wry look. 'Yeah, quite a turnaround

from his attempt to pay me to stay away from you, wasn't it?'

'I don't understand… How did you get in contact with my father?' she asked. 'He's been based in France for the last three months.'

'Well, here's where the coincidence occurred,' he said. 'I was giving a lecture in Paris. I literally ran into him on the street.'

'I don't suppose he shook your hand and wished you all the best,' Mikki said darkly.

'Actually, he did shake my hand and wish me all the best,' Lewis said. 'He also told me how worried he was about you.'

Mikki turned away and stomped back inside. 'So I suppose he let drop that Mum and I have dinner fortnightly at that restaurant so that you could conveniently be there to see for yourself what a heart-sore wreck I was.'

'He didn't exactly put it like that.'

She swung around to glare at him. 'How did he put it?'

Lewis held the challenging heat of her gaze. 'He felt it would be helpful if you and I met up and sorted out our differences once and for all. He thought you were having trouble moving on with your life. He thought if I saw you, it would help relieve some of the tension.'

Mikki folded her arms and gave him a scathing glare. 'What tension are we talking about here? And what exactly was the plan you cooked up between you? That you'd waltz back into my life and have a hot little fling with me to get me back on the horse, so to speak?'

'There was no plan. It wasn't my intention to get

involved with you again,' he said. 'I wasn't even going to go along with the restaurant thing but your father felt it would be better for you to see me for the first time away from the hospital. I could see the sense in that. I didn't want to be involved in some sort of a scene on my first day at a new hospital.'

Mikki paced the floor a couple of times. She was outraged by her father's intervention, but even more upset that Lewis had gone along with it. It made her feel as if he had only gone to the restaurant because he had been asked to go, not because he'd genuinely wanted to see her again. And even worse, he had decided to see her that night ostensibly to *protect* his precious career, to save himself from a scene with her on the ward! She cringed at how gullible she had been. She should have known it from the first moment she saw him sitting at that table. It was far too coincidental. And then Abby had shown up and he'd made no introductions, deliberately allowing her to think his half-sister was his new lover. She felt furious for falling in love with him when he had been playing a game set up by her father.

'Mikki, I think you're overreacting,' Lewis said. 'Your father was only trying to do what was best for you.'

She stopped pacing and threw him a cutting glare. 'So whose idea was it to get involved?' she asked. 'Yours or his?'

'The getting-involved thing...well, it just...happened.'

Mikki snatched up his keys from the coffee table where he had left them earlier. 'Then it can *un*happen,' she said. 'Get out. I don't want to see you unless it's at work. We're over.'

He took the keys without a word, his fingers closing over them as he moved past her to the door. She heard the door open and then close, the lock clicking like a punctuation mark being typed on a document. End of story.

CHAPTER TWELVE

'WERE you called in last night?' Jane asked the next morning.

'No. Why?' Mikki asked, running her eyes down Jenny Upton's file.

'You look like you haven't slept.' She swung back and forth on the chair. 'Or maybe a certain hot specialist was keeping you awake, having his wicked way with you, hmm?'

Mikki closed the file with a snap. 'I have patients to see,' she said, and stalked out.

Kylie was coming into the office as Mikki was leaving. 'Dr Landon?'

'What is it?' Mikki snapped.

'Mrs Yates just had a cardiac arrest.'

Mikki stood back from the patient's bed. 'Time of death ten twenty-five a.m.' She turned to the nurse on duty. 'I'll speak to the family. They'll want some time with her before she's transferred to the morgue.'

Mrs Yates's daughters were sad but relieved their mother was now at peace. Garry, however, was livid. He ranted and raved and accused Mikki of tampering with the ventilator.

'I am sorry for your loss, Mr Yates,' she said. 'But there was nothing we could do. Your mother's heart simply gave up.'

'You're not going to get away with this,' he stormed. 'I'm going to sue you for malpractice.'

'Nice piece of work,' Jane said as he left.

Mikki rolled her eyes wearily as she sat down. 'This day can't possibly get any worse.'

'Trouble with Lewis?' Jane asked.

Mikki tightened her mouth. 'I don't want to talk about it.'

'Talking might help,' Jane said.

'It won't.'

'Sad about Lewis's father,' Jane said. 'Fancy being estranged for eighteen years.'

Mikki stood up to leave. 'It's none of my business.'

Mikki went down to the medical ward, checking first that Lewis wasn't with his father before she went into Robert's room. Robert was lying with an open book on his chest. He had obviously grown too tired to hold it up to read.

'Hello, Mr Beck,' she said. 'Do you feel up to a visitor?'

He gave her a churlish look. 'Can't see why you'd bother.'

Mikki closed the door and came over to his bedside. 'It's a long day in hospital,' she said. 'An occasional visitor can make all the difference.'

'Won't make much difference to me,' he said. 'I'm still going to die.'

'We're all going to die,' she said.

He turned his head and looked at her, his eyes, apart from the whites being almost yellow, so like Lewis's she felt her heart take a little stumble. He turned away again and sighed.

'Did you know Lewis spent some time in Afghanistan?' she asked.

Robert looked at her again, his throat moving over a swallow. 'Was he…was he in any danger?'

'Two of his colleagues were killed in front of him,' Mikki said. 'He could have been killed too. He was lucky he wasn't but if he had been I would have had to spend the rest of my life knowing I could have contacted him and said sorry for running away, for not being mature enough to work through things.'

'How did you meet my son?' he asked after a brief silence.

Mikki took the chair by the bedside and told him how she had rushed into the pub to get out of the rain and had run into Lewis. 'He was so good about being speared in the stomach with my umbrella,' she said, smiling in nostalgia.

'So you fell in love,' Robert said, still looking at her.

Mikki chewed at her bottom lip, her colour rising. 'I think it was more a case of falling in lust,' she said. 'I was totally out of my depth. He was so handsome and charming when he put his mind to it. I was lonely so far away from home. But I loved him. I loved him desperately.'

'How long were you together?'

'Nine weeks, five days and eighteen hours,' she said.

The blue eyes were steady on hers. 'So what happened?'

'Hasn't Abby told you all this?' she asked.

'Yes, but I would like to hear it from you,' he said.

She looked down at her hands. 'I fell pregnant.'

'It happens.'

She looked up. 'Yes, but Lewis blamed himself. He insisted we marry. I didn't think we should rush into it but I let him talk me into it. The plans were all in place. My parents had flown over. But then I lost the baby. I was shocked at how disappointed I was. Most girls in my situation would have been relieved. I felt as if my heart had been cut out of me. But for some reason I couldn't talk to Lewis about it. And he didn't talk about it with me. He carried on as if nothing had happened. I was so angry at him. I started to hate him. I can't believe I could love someone so much and then hate them the next...'

The room felt as if it had suddenly sucked in a deep breath, the silence was so intense.

Mikki looked up to see two tears rolling down Robert's cheeks. 'I'm sorry,' she said softly.

He reached out a thin hand and she grasped it in hers. 'Don't be,' he said.

She looked down at their joined hands. 'I really love Lewis,' she confessed. 'But I don't know how to reach him.'

'You've come to the wrong person for advice,' Robert said with a touch of wryness. 'But, then, maybe we're too alike. My first wife, the boys' mother Claire, always said that's why I had so much trouble with Lewis.'

He looked at her again. 'You remind me of her. You have the same soft brown eyes and honey-brown hair.'

He looked away again, as if far into the distance. 'I've never forgiven myself for her death. What a fool I was.'

Mikki blinked back tears. 'We all have wisdom in hindsight. No one gets through life without making mistakes. Some are more costly than others.'

Robert tightened his hold on her hand. 'I really want to be close to my son. I blame myself for Liam's death. I should have been there that weekend. Lewis was just a kid. At sixteen what would he have known about head injuries? He did the right thing. He called an ambulance and he got him to the nearest hospital as soon as he could. He was there when I wasn't.' He put a hand to his face, a broken sob cracking his voice. 'Every time I look at Lewis, I see my own failings. I see how I let both of my boys down when they needed me most. I've pushed him away because he reminds me of all I'm not and can never be. And now it's too late.'

Mikki took his hand and held it close to her heart. 'It's never too late. I'm sure if you told Lewis what you felt, he would understand. He's a compassionate man, just like you. You hide it just like he does behind that I-don't-give-a-damn exterior. Just let him in. Drop your guard and I am sure he will drop his.'

He gave her a tired smile that spoke of years of sadness and regret. 'You're a nice girl,' he said. 'I wish I had more time to get to know you. I think you're perfect for Lewis. You're strong enough to stand up to him. Claire let me dominate her, so did Anna, Abby's mother. The last thing a Beck man needs is a doormat. We're the type of man who needs a woman who knows what she wants and goes out and gets it.'

'I can't quite see myself dragging Lewis back to my lair and insisting he does things my way,' Mikki said, thinking despondently of how she had sent him away so angrily the night before. He had left without another word. Surely if he had wanted her to stay involved with him, he would have said something? But, then, wasn't that what his father was saying? The Beck pride was their strength *and* their weakness.

'Maybe you should meet him halfway,' Robert said. 'I wish I had done that all those years ago.'

Mikki stayed talking to Robert for over an hour. He talked some more about the past and about Lewis and Liam as young boys. He even got her to get one of the nurses to unlock the drawer where his wallet had been placed for safekeeping. He opened it to show her a faded and much-crinkled photograph of Lewis and Liam as little boys. Lewis had his arm protectively around Liam's shoulder, a serious look on his face, while Liam was smiling broadly. The image told her more than words could ever do, so too did the way Robert carefully tucked it away once she handed it back as if it was his most priceless possession.

'Thanks for dropping by,' Robert said, clearly tired now.

She took his hand and held it gently in hers. 'I'll see you tomorrow. I hope you get a good night's rest.'

'In this place, with all those nurses bustling about and those junior doctors who look like they should still be in high school?' he said, but she could see he had a twinkle in his eye this time.

Mikki smiled, leaned down and kissed his cheek. 'You're a nice man, Robert. I'm so glad we've finally met.'

Lewis wandered among the gravestones towards his brother's resting place. The site right next to their mother's overlooked the ocean. That was the beauty of Waverly Cemetery. It formed part of the Bondi-to-Coogee Beach coastal walk, a walk he and his brother had done numerous times in search of perfect waves.

The grave was not as neglected as he had been expecting. Somehow he couldn't quite see his father coming out here and leaving flowers and weeding the site week after week, even month after month, but someone had been there only a day or so ago. He reached down and picked up the card loosely attached to the bunch of orange tulips placed in the polished brass vase. It read: 'With love, Dad.'

Lewis put the card back and straightened. His eyes went to the grave alongside. It too had a bunch of flowers and a card attached. He read his mother's name on the gravestone and the Bible verse that was supposed to define her life but somehow didn't. He plucked the card from the flowers and read: 'Forgive me.'

A tight feeling cramped his chest and he turned to look at the surging ocean in the distance. A slim figure was walking along the track that followed the boundary of the cemetery. He narrowed his eyes and his chest tightened a bit further as the female figure looked up and sighted him.

He watched her make her way up through the lives and histories of the past. It was symbolic in a way. So many lives, so many losses, so much grief, but at the end of it he was waiting for her.

'How did you know I was here?' Lewis asked as Mikki came to stand in front of his brother's resting place.

'It seemed the logical place you would be,' she said.

She bent down and put some bright yellow daffodils beside the tulips. 'I thought it was high time I met the rest of your family.'

'This is Liam,' Lewis said. 'And next to him is our mother.'

'Hi, I'm Michaela Landon,' she said, addressing the graves. 'But only my parents call me that. Everyone else calls me Mikki.'

The silence was broken by the lonely cry of a seagull as it flew overhead.

'Mikki, I feel bad about leaving you last night,' Lewis said. 'I should have insisted on staying and working things out. I'm always criticising you for running away and yet I did it myself. What a hypocrite.'

'It's all right,' she said. 'You needed your space. I understand that about you now. It's taken me a long time but I get it, finally.'

He looked out at the ocean for a long moment without speaking. His face was unreadable, but she could see his throat rise and fall over a swallow.

'Your father wants to see you,' she said into the silence.

Lewis curled his lip. 'Yeah, well, he can forget about it. I'm not putting my head on the block again.'

'He loves you, Lewis. He really does. He's just not so good at showing it.'

He bent down and pulled a few stray weeds out from between the marble plinths. 'I suppose he wants me to go in there and grovel, to beg for forgiveness when for all this time he's the one who should have been apologising to me.'

'Actually, I think he wants you to ask me to marry you.'

'As if I'm going to go in there and beg him for anything,' he went on, pulling at the weeds with unnecessary force. 'He's a stubborn old fool who can't see what's right under his nose.'

'Yes, well, you know what they say: like father, like son,' Mikki said.

Lewis's hand stilled on the milk thistle he was about to rip out by the roots. He looked up over his shoulder at Mikki. 'He wants me to *what*?'

She waited until he straightened before she answered. 'He thinks you love me.'

'Why's that?' he asked, the mask still in place on his face.

'I think he believes you are still madly in love with me but are too stupid or too stubborn or both to admit it,' she said.

Lewis tilted his head as he studied her. 'What did you say to that?' he asked.

'I told him I still love you, that I haven't stopped loving you in spite of all the years that have passed, that when I think of how you could have died in Afghanistan, my life would have ended too if you had. I would have never recovered. I can't live without you. I don't want to live without you.'

He looked at her in shocked silence.

'I thought I would come and find you, talk to you instead of storming off in a huff, as is my usual practice,' she said. 'I thought I should tell you again that I love you. You didn't want to hear it the other day but I need to tell you again anyway. I love you so much I can't bear the thought of missing out on another seven minutes of time together, let alone seven years. I thought I would tell you that it doesn't matter that my father interfered, and my mother too, when it comes to that. All that matters is I want to be with you and only you.'

A slow smile started in his eyes and finally lifted up the corners of his mouth. 'Isn't it the man's job to do the proposing?' he asked.

'You did it the last time,' Mikki said. 'And look where that got us.'

He rubbed at his jaw. 'Yeah, you're right. It was a pretty lousy proposal if I remember. Maybe I should have another shot at it.'

'Feel free,' she said with a widening smile.

Lewis swept his gaze around their surroundings. 'I wonder if anyone has been proposed to in a graveyard before?' he mused.

'I don't know,' Mikki said. 'I guess it's not the most romantic place but at least your mum and your brother can be the first to hear my answer.'

Lewis took her hands in his, holding them close to his chest. He took a steadying breath; his heart beating so hard Mikki could feel it against her fingers. 'I love you, Mikki,' he said. 'I hadn't realised how much until just lately. I never wanted to fall in love. I never wanted to feel the pain again of losing someone I loved. I guess that's why I always held myself back from you. I gave you so little of myself. When you walked away after losing the baby I let you go. Looking back, I think it was because I didn't want you to see how much I wanted you to stay. I did it again last night. I just walked away. I was just too proud to say what I really wanted to say.'

Mikki looked up at him in remorse. 'That was my fault last night. I was angry about my father setting things up. It made me feel as if you had been lying to me right from the start. That you were only having a relationship with me for the sake of getting some closure, not because you wanted to be with me more than anything.'

Lewis tightened his hold on her hands. 'Will you marry me, Mikki?' he asked. 'Will you be my wife and the mother of my babies?'

Mikki's eyes misted. 'You want to have babies?'

He smiled all the way up to his eyes. 'Yeah, I think I do. Two or maybe three. What do you think?'

She smiled with elation. 'I think that's a wonderful plan. When can we get started?'

'Hey,' he said, putting on a mock frown. 'Hold your horses, young lady. We're going to do things the right way around this time—the old-fashioned way. I'm not getting you pregnant until I get a ring on your finger. So you'd better tell me one way or the other if you're going to say yes to my proposal.'

Mikki nestled up close, looking up at him with all the love she felt for him shining in her eyes. 'Yes,' she said. 'A thousand trillion squillion times yes.'

Lewis smiled and looked down at his brother and mother's graves. 'Did you hear that, Mum and Liam?' he said. 'We're getting married.'

Three months later...

Lewis wheeled his father's chair out onto the balcony of his house so he could watch the dolphins playing in the surf. 'Is there anything I can get you, Dad?' he asked. 'Another drink or something to eat?'

Robert smiled and put his hand over his son's. 'No, I'm doing just fine, son. Mikki's been fussing over me non-stop.'

'I'm glad you made it to the wedding,' Lewis said. 'Now all you've got to do is try and make it to the christening.'

Robert looked up. 'What christening?'

Lewis smiled proudly. 'Mikki's having a baby. She conceived on our honeymoon.'

Robert's eyes watered up as his reached for Lewis's hand again. 'You've made me very proud, Lewis,' he said. 'I can't tell you how proud. Your mother would be so happy for you. Liam too.'

'I just want you to be happy, Dad,' Lewis said, 'happy and at peace.'

Mikki came out with a blanket to put over Robert's knees. 'Did Lewis tell you our news, Robert?'

'He did, and I couldn't be happier for you both.'

Lewis put his arm around his wife's waist. He couldn't wait to feel her body bloom further with pregnancy. She already had that wonderful glow about her. She had passed the time of the last miscarriage and the pregnancy was progressing well. He was thrilled at the prospect of becoming a father. Mikki had surprised him by insisting on knowing the sex. He had thought she would want to be surprised as a lot of first-time mums did. But for his father's sake she had wanted to know. That had really touched Lewis.

'Robert, we're having a son,' Mikki said, smiling.

'A son, hey?' Robert said with an answering smile. 'Have you thought of names?'

'Yes,' Lewis said. 'Liam Robert.'

Robert reached for Lewis's hand, his eyes watering up again. 'Thank you, son. And thank you, Mikki.'

'I bet he's going to be stubborn and proud, like his father and grandfather,' Mikki said, still smiling.

'He wouldn't be a Beck if he wasn't.' Lewis grinned back.

The last three months had seen such a turnaround in Lewis's life. His relationship with his father had taken some time to repair. There had been years of hurts and misunderstandings to wade through, but together they had done it and now were both determined to enjoy what time they had left. It was a poignant time, helping his father face the end of his life, but Lewis had learned a lot about his father in the process. And had learned a lot about himself. He had learned about love and forgiveness and letting go, but, even more important, holding onto what really mattered.

Mikki mattered.

He looked down at her nestled up against him so trustingly, so full of love for him it made his heart swell

like the surf below. It had taken him seven long, lonely
years to realise it, but Mikki mattered to him more than
anything in the world.

Book of the Month

MODERN

MAISEY YATES
The Highest Price to Pay

BOOK
OF THE
MONTH

We love this book because...

Maisey Yates has an incredible talent for writing intense, emotional romance with a sexy, sassy edge. In *The Highest Price to Pay*, she creates a world of high fashion and even higher stakes!

On sale 15th July

Visit us Online

Find out more at
www.millsandboon.co.uk/BOTM

0711/03a

CAREER GIRL IN THE COUNTRY
by Fiona Lowe

Dynamic city surgeon Poppy can't believe she's been sent to work in the rural Outback! Her gorgeous colleague, emergency doctor Matt, thrives on the small-town solitude, but Poppy knows he's hiding from something…and she's determined to make him face his secrets!

THE DOCTOR'S REASON TO STAY
by Dianne Drake

After finding his little ward Molly the loving parents he never had, brooding surgeon Dr Rafe Corbett intends to leave town for good. Edie Parker intends to make Rafe realise *he* is the father Molly needs. But can she convince him to stay—because Edie is losing her heart to them both…

WEDDING ON THE BABY WARD
by Lucy Clark

Determined to deliver her best friend's precious twins safely, Dr Janessa Austen calls on neonatal specialist Miles Trevellion's expertise. These tiny baby girls must be Miles' *only* priority—the beautiful Janessa can be nothing more than his colleague. For now…

SPECIAL CARE BABY MIRACLE
by Lucy Clark

New mum Sheena's newborn girls are fighting for their lives and paediatric surgeon Will Beckman is the man to save them—the same Will who was once the love of Sheena's life! Sheena's hoping for two little miracles—but perhaps an unexpected third dream might also come true?

On sale from 5th August 2011
Don't miss out!

Available at WHSmith, Tesco, ASDA, Eason and all good bookshops
www.millsandboon.co.uk

Medical Romance™

THE TORTURED REBEL
by Alison Roberts

Beautiful helicopter pilot Becca Harding has spent long years trying to forget SAS medic and emergency specialist Jet Munroe, but she's never been able to forgive him. Now, thrown together again, it's time to stop running from their past, and the scorching attraction still lingering between them.

DATING DR DELICIOUS
by Laura Iding

It's Hannah Stewart's first day as a surgical intern at Chicago's busiest hospital and she couldn't be more excited—then she meets Dr Jake Holt, her new boss...the man she had a completely out-of-character, one-night stand with! Jake has a strict "no relationships at work" rule, but his new intern is proving to be a distraction impossible to ignore...!

**On sale from 5th August 2011
Don't miss out!**

Available at WHSmith, Tesco, ASDA, Eason and all good bookshops
www.millsandboon.co.uk

2 FREE BOOKS
AND A SURPRISE GIFT

We would like to take this opportunity to thank you for reading this Mills & Boon® book by offering you the chance to take TWO more specially selected books from the Medical™ series absolutely FREE! We're also making this offer to introduce you to the benefits of the Mills & Boon® Book Club™—

- **FREE home delivery**
- **FREE gifts and competitions**
- **FREE monthly Newsletter**
- **Exclusive Mills & Boon Book Club offers**
- **Books available before they're in the shops**

Accepting these FREE books and gift places you under no obligation to buy, you may cancel at any time, even after receiving your free books. Simply complete your details below and return the entire page to the address below. You don't even need a stamp!

YES Please send me 2 free Medical books and a surprise gift. I understand that unless you hear from me, I will receive 5 superb new stories every month including two 2-in-1 books priced at £5.30 each and a single book priced at £3.30, postage and packing free. I am under no obligation to purchase any books and may cancel my subscription at any time. The free books and gift will be mine to keep in any case.

Ms/Mrs/Miss/Mr _____ Initials _____

Surname _____

Address _____

_____ Postcode _____

E-mail _____

Send this whole page to: Mills & Boon Book Club, Free Book Offer, FREEPOST NAT 10298, Richmond, TW9 1BR

Offer valid in UK only and is not available to current Mills & Boon Book Club subscribers to this series. Overseas and Eire please write for details. We reserve the right to refuse an application and applicants must be aged 18 years or over. Only one application per household. Terms and prices subject to change without notice. Offer expires 30th September 2011. As a result of this application, you may receive offers from Harlequin (UK) and other carefully selected companies. If you would prefer not to share in this opportunity please write to The Data Manager, PO Box 676, Richmond, TW9 1WU.

Mills & Boon® is a registered trademark owned by Harlequin (UK) Limited.
Medical™ is being used as a trademark. The Mills & Boon® Book Club™ is being used as a trademark.